Reckless Appetites

Reckless Appetites

a culinary romance

Jacqueline Deval

The Ecco Press

Copyright © 1993 by Jacqueline Deval
All rights reserved

Published by The Ecco Press in 1993
100 West Broad Street, Hopewell, NJ 08525
Published simultaneously in Canada by
Penguin Books Canada Ltd., Ontario
Printed in the United States of America

Library of Congress Cataloging-in-Publication Data
Deval, Jacqueline.
Reckless appetites : a culinary romance / by Jacqueline Deval.—
1st ed.
     p.   cm.
     Includes bibliographical references and index.
ISBN 0-88001-322-2
1. Young women—England—London—Fiction.   2. Man-woman
relationships—Fiction.   3. Cookery—Fiction.   4. Cookery.
I. Title.
PS3554.E922R43   1993   93-22175
813'.54—dc20   CIP

Designed by Barbara Cohen Aronica

FIRST EDITION

The text of this book is set in 10½/14 Simoncini Garamond

For Bill and Jean Deval

ACKNOWLEDGMENTS

My special thanks to readers and friends Loretta Barrett, Richard Eder, Lynn Goldberg, Dan Halpern, Kelvin Christopher James, Jeanne Krier, Susan Randol, and Laura Van Wormer.

CONTENTS

THE CHARACTERS

Pomme Bouquin, a young woman, a reader and a cook

Jeremy, Pomme's lover in London

*Henri Bouquin, Pomme's father, a chef at
London's Savoy Hotel*

Étienne Sansigne, Henri's friend, a chef in Paris

The Professor, Pomme's lover in America

CHAPTER ONE

Passionate Tastes

POMME'S SEDUCTION

If one wished to be perfectly sincere, one would
have to admit there are two kinds of love—well-fed
and ill-fed. The rest is pure fiction.

—Colette

All human history attests
That happiness for man—the hungry sinner!
Since Eve ate apples, much depends on dinner.

—Byron

*I*magine a woman. Her name is Pomme. She is in love,
alone in her room, but not lonely. She is spending the
evening with Colette in mind, seeking the secrets of her
own appetite. Pomme's intended lover, Jeremy, has resisted her,
cautious before plunging into the turmoil of a passionate affair. The
excruciating pace—so painfully slow—has her in a perpetual and
exquisite state of anticipation. "Will he or won't he?" she demands
aloud to herself, to Colette. "How can I have him?" Like the young
woman who frequents an opium den in one of Colette's stories,
Pomme breathes in the black, appetizing aroma of fresh truffles or

burnt cocoa, hoping to find comfort in the heady sensation of patience, optimism, and a vague hunger. Tonight, under Colette's guidance, she'll slake her desire by planning the dinner she will prepare for Jeremy. A most important meal.

Reading Colette is a voluptuous experience for Pomme, filled with the sights and sounds and tastes of Paris, of food, of men. She leaves Pomme feeling oddly out of time, like a woman in a Romantic painting, breathless and prone on an overstuffed sofa while her lover bestows his first kiss. Colette's fruits are heavy, full, and scented. Her chocolate is melted and hot and enticing. Her cheeses and truffles, chosen so carefully, augur culinary ecstasy. Colette's descriptions of food rouse a heightened awareness of the power of the senses. For Colette, "divining a cheese," probing its elasticity, the fissures in its rind, determining whether the "pearly distillation from a Munster is too liquid and holds a promise of premature bitterness," are tests of womanhood. Colette once said that if she had a son of marriageable age, she would warn him to beware of young women who love neither wine nor truffles nor cheese nor music.

Pomme stirs from her bed where she has been reading Colette's amorous and culinary adventures, determined to devote what she has learned to her own life of love. Like her namesake, a precocious schoolgirl who appears in Colette's *Claudine Married,* Pomme's awareness of her own seductive prowess is dawning only slowly. "Pomme! Someone'll eat her up with a name like that," says a man taken with the fictional Pomme's charm. The smell of cinnamon clings to Pomme, a warm exotic smell, a scent that Jeremy has already breathed in deeply, greedily, surreptitiously. He has been startled by the generosity in her widemouthed smile, the frankness in her open, heart-shaped face. He is amused by her disregard for her appearance, her clothing sometimes splattered with cooking stains, her thick braid often losing its strands. He hides the signs of Pomme's disturbing effect on him.

While Colette, who made a career of observing nature and the ways of love, will share a recipe or two, Pomme will consult others who have talked about food and love. "I have too much to learn too quickly," she murmurs, hoping that her serendipitous excursions through writers' lives of love will show her what to do. When writers have anticipated an evening of seduction, did they plan the event as carefully as they would a novel? After all, creating the right atmosphere, an air that fairly hums with tension, is crucial. The setting of the table and the scene also is critical to the evening's outcome. And if the seduction failed, have writers consoled themselves in the knowledge that at least they can use insights gleaned as material for the next book? Do writers ever stop working?

Pomme creates splendid meals and aspires to become a celebrated chef, like her father. She practices her art with joyful determination. When she is not in her kitchen, she is reading, her romantic tastes shaped by her mother, a woman who takes her pleasure in the vast reading rooms of magnificent libraries. Pomme has learned from cooking and literature that the finest seduction engages all the senses. At a meal designed to allure, the rising scent from an intensely fragrant dish should mingle with an increasing air of celebration, like the boeuf en daube in Virginia Woolf's *To the Lighthouse*. The conversation between lovers over dinner is also vital. Which foods will bring out the right talk, the revelations of personal histories that lead a pair into love?

The meal, neither heavy nor distracting nor difficult to eat, should further the evening's purpose. The wrong food might destroy romance. Mrs. Waters in Fielding's *Tom Jones* knew this well when the vast piece of beef and bubbling ale distracted Tom from her penetrating glances and desirous sighs. Love should provoke laughter, both light and serious. Food must not weigh those efforts down. Mrs. Waters won by persistence, disarming Tom with smiles and glances brimming with significance, but only after the dinner had been cleared away. Mrs. Charles Dickens, less successful at the dinner table, experienced amatory disaster. In *What Shall We Have for Dinner?* she promised readers that her cookbook would help keep husbands at home with its recipes for potato balls (baked balls of mashed potato) and reheated codfish—"Take any cold cod that may be left, warm up with mashed potatoes, and serve with oyster sauce poured over." Even though the cod arrived on the Dickens dinner table as cod *rechauffé,* Dickens left his wife for a young actress, causing a public scandal. "I will avoid cod *rechauffé* at all costs," Pomme vows. "But which other writers shall I petition? Who will even begin to answer my thousand questions about food, about love?"

Pomme must choose her mentors well. "I shall always be a priest of love," D. H. Lawrence once wrote, making Pomme suspicious of his self-congratulatory expertise. What kind of love affair would he imagine for her? She has only to look at his illustration for *Venus in the Kitchen,* a semisatiric aphrodisiac cookbook by novelist Norman Douglas, to recognize Lawrence's depraved view of love. The somber drawing shows a naked couple baking bread, the woman shoveling a loaf of bread into an open flaming oven while her lover clutches her awkwardly from behind. They are out of proportion, lumpy, grotesque. Douglas's introduction declares that D. H. Lawrence looked as if his own health would have been improved by the book's aphrodisiac recipes. Graham Greene, master of the guilt-laden and doomed literary love affair, contributed the preface and praised the book's "air of scholarship, its blend of the practical—the almond soup—and the wildly impractical—Roti sans Pareil, the crispness of the comments."

Such odd advice, Pomme reflects, as she reads *Venus in the*

Kitchen's recipes for caviar and oysters—spiced, raw, or stewed in ways designed to seduce. The startling array of foods, calculated to drive one into the author's lusting embrace, makes Pomme feel ill in the contemplation. Dishes made from eels, kidneys, brains, and pies calling for bull's testicles, are described in conspiratorial tones with a knowing nod to anyone who's watching. *Venus in the Kitchen* conjures all too clearly the image of the author's ropey old arm wrapped around a tender young thing, unaware of how foolish he looks, slyly winking to the maître d'hôtel, urging his victim back to his room, where he has a plate of bull testicle pie ready to spring the trap. Pomme imagines peeling his insistent arms from her neck and flying back to Colette's comforting embrace and wise words.

Pomme thinks about Colette's Claudine, alone and melancholy, waiting breathlessly for her life to begin, pining for a future partly veiled, sensing that something important lies just ahead, but what is it precisely and when will it be here? Pomme and Claudine are on the brink of their lives, missing what they've not yet experienced, entangled in the impatience of their youth. Pomme reads Colette's words aloud, tasting chocolate and solitude, as Colette describes Claudine sitting by the fire:

> Whoever would have believed that she was revolving such tearful thoughts, this Claudine, squatting cross-legged in a dressing-gown before the marble chimneypiece and apparently completely absorbed in roasting one side of a bar of chocolate kept upright between a pair of tongs? When the surface exposed to the fire softened, blackened, crackled and blistered, I lifted it off in thin layers with my little knife. . . . Exquisite taste, a mixture of grilled almonds and grated vanilla! The melancholy sweetness of savoring the toasted chocolate. . . .

Pomme's vision of Claudine settles the question of dessert for Jeremy's dinner—melted chocolate, delicately warmed over a flame, in which to dip fresh black cherries, the first of the season. Colette once talked about cherries that had been warmed on the tree. "It is not in your mouth but in mine that they melt so deliciously now," she wrote to an absent lover. Unlike Claudine and Colette, who tasted their chocolate and cherries alone, Pomme and Jeremy will make the dessert together, mutually concentrating on the sweet task at hand.

When Madame de Sévigné wrote that chocolate "pleases you for a little while, but then all of a sudden it kindles a mortal fever in you," she sensed what scientists have since speculated upon—a chemical connection between the desires for chocolate and for love. Does consuming chocolate stimulate falling in love? In case the answer one day proves to be yes, Pomme will enlist science on her side.

When Pomme saw Jeremy for the first time, he was reading Lord Byron's *Don Juan.* She dreams of the poet sailing in a gondola down the Grand Canal with his Venetian mistress, eating from the ball of polenta she kept warm between her breasts. Byron wrote to a friend:

> As to "Don Juan," confess—confess—you dog—and be candid—that it is the sublime of *that there* sort of writing—it may be bawdy—but is it not good English?—it may be profligate—but is it not *life,* is it not *the thing*—Could any man have written it—who has not lived in the world?—and tooled in a post-chaise?—in a hackney coach?—in a Gondola?—against a wall? . . . —on a table?—and under it?

"Must I buy plane tickets to Venice, taking a recipe for polenta with me?" Pomme muses, half seriously, knowing that the idea of someone lodging polenta between her breasts requires further investigation, if only from a logical point of view. Polenta, made from cornmeal, can be served hot and creamy immediately after cooking, or cooled and sliced like cake. Pomme smiles at the idea of experimenting to find just the right consistency,[1] but doubts Byron's amorous expertise, the clash between his yearning for pure love and his insatiable lust. One letter in particular makes him the most unsuitable champion of her cause. On September 25, 1812, he wrote to Lady Melbourne, the aunt of his future bride, about another lover:

> She besides does not speak English, and to me nothing but Italian, a great point, for certain coincidences the very sound of that language is Music to me, and she has black eyes and not a very white skin, and reminds me of many in the Archipelago I wish to forget, and makes me forget what I ought to remember, all which are against me.—I only wish she did not swallow so much supper, chicken wings—sweet breads,—custards—peaches & Port wine—a woman should never be seen eating or drinking, unless it be a lobster sallad and Champagne, the only truly feminine and becoming viands.

Pomme is in trouble if Jeremy believes in Byron. She likes to eat and does not like lobster, a difficult and distracting food. Pomme knows that lobster's appearance in Colette's fiction bodes ill for romance. Léa in *Chéri* served a lobster dinner to commemorate the loss of her lover—what a falsely cheerful meal that must have been. In *Mitsou,* the lovers dined on lobster à l'Indienne, a meal that revealed only Mitsou's blithe lack of taste and knowledge. The evening left a bitter flavor in her lover's mouth. He no longer wanted her.

Byron, in his abhorrence of watching women eat, interrogated his hosts before he accepted an invitation to make sure no women would be among the guests. He once turned down a dinner because Madame de Staël, the writer and critic, had also been invited. Fickle, self-absorbed, and syphilitic to boot, Byron with his advice on love is not to be trusted. Does Pomme dare to dismiss one of history's great lovers in so cavalier a fashion? *Mais, bien sûr!* cries out Colette. All great seducers are treacherous, Colette declares— something she once said about a bottle of wine but which applies to Byron too. Colette once asked a self-styled, modern-day Don Juan about the memory he had left with the women he had possessed. "Why, without a doubt," he replied without a moment's hesitation, "a feeling of not having had quite enough." Like Colette's heroines, with their natural, animal-like enjoyment of food, Pomme decides to feed her lover full and to take her full share too.

Pomme reads the love letters of other writers, looking for their experiences of dinnertime seductions. In a letter to his beloved Sarah Stoddard, William Hazlitt revealed an honesty of feelings that boded for a terminally dull marriage. Although he praised the tingle in her cheeks, Hazlitt declared that he loved her best when they dined together on a broiled scragg-end of mutton and hot potatoes. Sarah and William eventually married and eventually divorced. Perhaps Sarah didn't care for scragg-ends, or for his instructive comments that appeared later in the letter about how she should wear her hair. When Pomme strays from Colette, she discovers only what not to serve at dinner. Byron would have her serve lobster or else nothing for herself; Hazlitt, an ugly cut of meat and potatoes; the Dickens household, some reheated codfish; Greene, D. H. Lawrence, and Norman Douglas, eel or testicle pie.

Among the French, who consider romance and food as national treasures, Pomme will seek the generous, full flavors she needs. Surely, Gustave Flaubert, who wrote of Emma Bovary's yearnings, understood desire better than the British poets and writers. But then he too quickly disappoints with his "appetites of wild beasts, the instinct of a love that is carnivorous, capable of tearing flesh to pieces. Is this love? Perhaps it is the opposite. Perhaps in my case it's the heart that's impotent." When Flaubert's lover, Louise Colet, received that letter, did she finally understand how deeply he believed that the satisfaction of the body and the head have nothing in common? Possibly Flaubert wrote the letter after one of his literary dinner parties, where he often boasted about his many and varied sexual conquests. For him, not unlike Byron, lust had little to do with a higher spiritual satisfaction that he declared attainable for him only through art.

At a dinner with Flaubert in 1860, Edmond and Jules de Goncourt discussed the various merits of all the actresses they knew. "Flaubert gave us his recipe for possessing them: you have to be sentimental and take them seriously." On another occasion, Flaubert tells them that he had used all the women he had ever had as mattresses for another woman—the woman of his dreams. He had also found a way to do without women: "I just lie face down, and during the night . . . it's infallible."

"Women and love, these are always the subjects of conversation among intelligent men eating and drinking together," Edmond de Goncourt noted in his journal, going on cheerfully to say that the talk became filthy and depraved during the evening of January 28, 1878. "Flaubert makes himself out to be the most passionate man in the world," Goncourt wrote, "but in fact his friends have always known that woman plays a relatively minor part in his life." The divorce of lust and love that Flaubert implies depresses Pomme. She suddenly remembers that, in the end, Flaubert had Emma Bovary commit suicide by poison.

As for the Goncourt brothers, they intrigue Pomme with their account of April 24, 1858, when at dinner "between the chocolate soufflé and the chartreuse Maria loosened her corsets and began the story of her life," leaving the reader to speculate what happened next. Maria may have loosened her corsets, but the brothers believed in the purity of brotherly love and regarded women with stony suspicion. They spluttered indignantly upon discovering that Rose, their recently deceased cook and housekeeper who had baked apple turnovers for them when they were children, had been stealing from them for years, doling out household money, wines, and food to her lovers. While in their employ, Rose became pregnant and went to the hospital to have her baby. The Goncourt brothers, who saw Rose daily, never noticed a thing.

Their acquaintance Guy de Maupassant addressed the idea of food and love as related passions in a correspondence designed to impress a young woman, Marie Birktsheff, who had sent him a flirtatious fan letter:

> I put a good dinner, a real dinner, the rare dinner, almost in
> the same rank with a pretty woman. I think that when one
> has a good passion, a capital passion, one must give it full
> swing, must sacrifice all others to it. That is what I do. I had
> two passions. It was necessary to sacrifice one—I have to
> some extent sacrificed gluttony. I have become sober as a
> camel, but dainty in no longer knowing what to eat.

The dyspeptic rumblings of an old complainer must have chilled the woman's heart. After receiving a third letter from Maupassant, she severed all further contact.

"These Frenchmen will never do," Pomme sighs. "Romantic in inclination, ineffective in execution, they have no real strength. They are not like the man I want." She can almost hear Colette telling them, crossly, to stop being so literary. No, what Pomme seeks is that delicious marriage between literature and life that simply cannot be forced, but which can be persuaded, gently, to happen.

With a gentle tug, Colette leads Pomme home where the food is simple, the meals assembled from honest flavors. Those who partake give themselves over to indulging the most fundamental of all appetites, making the experience seem exotic even as the food they are eating is not. Colette's own favorite supper at one point in her life—a model of simplicity—was "a big wedge of cheese with the knob of a round loaf and a glass of red wine." As for her meals of love, they too are simple and good. They too demand surrender.

Colette decried the trend in France toward an overambitious, falsely nostalgic cuisine, a form of snobbery perverting the French people's appreciation of good food. "Be wary of those old grandmothers who suddenly, after half a century of modest silence in their graves, assume an importance in the dining room which nothing up to that point had led you to expect, and spring to life again around a dish of hare and rutabagas," she warned. She despised recipes that submerge the flavors of the prized Perigord truffle in grease, foie gras, and sauces. Why, she asked, can't we just love the truffle for itself? "Eat it on its own," she wrote, "scented and grainy-skinned, eat it like the vegetable it is, hot, and served in munificent quantities. Once scraped, it won't give you much trouble; its sovereign flavor disdains all complications and complicities."

Truffles. The very idea of them, their rarity, appeals to Pomme. They are an event, a food that lends an air of luxury to any meal. The first truffle eaters, citizens of fourteenth-century France, believed that truffles enhanced love. In those days, nearly every new food was considered an aphrodisiac, although the truffle never quite shook off that lovely reputation. Centuries later, French cooks served Sole Casanova, poached and laced with truffles, oysters, and mussels. A quick look through Casanova's autobiography shows Pomme that inspiration is not to be found in the literature of pornography, no matter how spicy. Casanova's pursuits center entirely on instant gratification and thoughts of the next conquest. He may have enjoyed pâtés, truffles, and oysters washed down with great draughts of frothy chocolate that he endorsed as an effective restorative, but his life seems loveless all the same. By the end of his days, food provided his one remaining pleasure. "At 73, no longer a god in the garden or a satyr in the forest, he is a wolf at the table," said one who knew him. Like Casanova, Napoleon recommended truffles as aphrodisiacs, but his opinion too is suspect. If Napoleon served truffles to a sensible courtesan, she'd naturally do her utmost to guarantee their success for him. The philosopher of the nineteenth-century kitchen, Anthelme Brillat-Savarin, claimed to have conducted experiments among his friends and acquaintances—both men and women—to examine the aphrodisiac quality of truffles. His conclusion: "The truffle is not a positive aphrodisiac, but it can upon occasion make women tenderer and men more apt to love."

The truffle itself does not provoke a loving reaction. More important is the atmosphere that the food helps to create. Any dish that has a method of preparation called Rêve d'Amour, or Dream of Love, has to be the right one to serve. Truffles à la Rêve d'Amour are cooked in champagne with herbs for twenty-five minutes and left to cool in the stock for twenty-four hours. But Pomme prefers Colette's recipe in *Earthly Paradise*. Truffles enhance the appetite, Colette says, so Pomme will serve them as an hors d'oeuvre.

Bathed in a very good dry white wine—keep the champagne for your banquets, the truffle can do without it—salted without extravagance, peppered with discretion, they can be cooked in a simple, black, cast-iron stewpan with the lid on. For twenty-five minutes, they must dance in the constant flow of bubbles, drawing with them through the eddies and the foam—like tritons playing around some darker Amphitrite—a score or so of smallish strips of bacon, fat, but not too fat, which will give body to the stock. No other herbs or spices! . . . Your truffles must come to the table in their own stock. Do not stint when you serve yourself.

Maurice Goudeket recalled in his memoirs the pleasure of eating truffles with his wife, Colette. He loved her deeply, frankly and unembarrassedly so, and his testimony makes Pomme fully confident in her choice of appetizer. Colette considered the cleaning of truffles an art and entrusted the task to no one, said Goudeket. "A divine and slightly suspect odor, like everything that smells really good, floats through the house. . . . Anyone who does not declare himself ready to leave Paradise or Hell for such a treat is not worthy to be born again."

Goudeket's own recipe calls for half a bottle of champagne, pieces of lightly browned bacon fat, salt and pepper, all boiled together before the truffles are added to the pan. "The scented sauce is served separately, hot in port glasses," he said.

Wine, preferably a Burgundy of impeccable ancestry or else the wine of Mercurey, full-bodied and velvety, must accompany truffles. About this, Colette was adamant. "Drink only a little, if you please. In the region where I was born, we always say that during a good meal one is not thirsty but hungry for wine." She advises a "familiar and discreet use of wine, not gulped down greedily but measured out into narrow glasses, assimilated mouthful by spaced-out, meditative mouthful."

For her entrée, Pomme returns to Claudine's first romantic

meal when she was a fresh, urgent country girl at dinner with an older man, far more experienced at seduction than she. The Asti, the peppered shrimp, the hard glitter of a chic Parisian restaurant, cast an intoxicating atmosphere, but it is the presence, "that almost black gaze with the lights shining in it," of the silver-streaked gentleman who could not take his eyes from her that freed Claudine from her fears. She surprised him with her open, hungry behavior. The peppered shrimp played their part well in that seduction, although later Claudine endured an unhappy marriage, a confining marriage, one in which her husband treated her as a child. No, shrimp are simply too close to their gloomy cousin, the lobster.

Instead Pomme looks to Colette's more mature Léa, borrowing Léa's way of enticing her young lover to the country with promises of broiled spring chicken, ripe strawberries, fresh cakes and cream. Broiled chicken appeared on Colette's own table, a dish she had prepared for Valère Vial, a man she described in *The Break of Day.* The book is at once a novel and a memoir, a coincidence of Colette's fiction and Colette's life, the boundaries utterly blurred.

Vial brought melons, an almond tart, and peaches to Colette at her seaside home in Saint-Tropez. Along with the young chickens, Colette planned to serve salads, a stuffed fish, and aubergine fritters, cooked à la Provençale in olive oil and garlic and sprinkled with parsley. "Four little chickens split in half, beaten with the flat of the chopper, salted, peppered, and anointed with pure oil brushed on with a sprig of pebreda. The little leaves of the pebreda, and the taste of it, cling to the grilled flesh," she wrote. Pebreda is one of the many pungent aromatic herbs that thrive in the dry hills of inland Provence. "Don't they look good?" Colette asked Vial. Vial was in love with her, but Colette was creating a life independent of love, although she enjoyed the possibility of succumbing to her own seduction.

Colette had Vial tie her apron, began to prepare a sharp, unctuous sauce, and told Vial to dip in his fingertip to try it. She instructed him to pour out some oil. "When I said 'Stop!' he cut short the thread of golden oil and straightened himself, and I laid my hand caressingly for a moment on his chest." She looked at her hand resting lightly on his body, proud of her homey and writerly strength, aware of her power over him. Vial licked her shoulder to see if she was salty from the sea. Even so, she knew she would resist him.

When she wrote *The Break of Day*, Colette was living in a house called La Treille Muscate, surrounded by four acres of land brimming with oranges, figs, garlic, pimentos, aubergines, peppers, and tomatoes and a scented garden of herbs and flowers. Pomme will pick a ruby ripe tomato from Colette's garden and serve it sliced with a sprinkling of vinaigrette and a few leaves of basil. Although olive oil, tomato, and garlic are the three staples of Provençale cooking, Colette never specified the sauce she prepared for the grilled chicken. The tomatoes might then be transformed into a sauce Provençale for the young chickens, cooked in oil with chopped onions and crushed garlic, seasoned with salt and pepper and parsley, white wine, and veal bouillon. Perhaps Pomme will also pick the cherries for her dessert from Colette's garden.

Another love scene, although it is not Colette's, piques Pomme's appetite. In a memoir, *The Big Sea*, Langston Hughes revealed his devotion to Anne Marie Coussey, a British-educated African woman who visited Paris to learn French and to escape an unfortunate engagement. On the eve of Anne's return to London, the lovers found a secluded restaurant in the Place du Tertre, almost at the top of one of those winding cobbled streets of Montmartre. There they drank wine and ate épaule de veau, salade de saison, and coeur à la crême, a heart-shaped mold of cream cheese served with strawberries and thin crisp cookies.

And then we went walking down the winding old streets of the hill, and across the Boulevard Clichy, and somehow we come to my house, and we went climbing up the steep stairs in the cool, half-dark hall, up, up, up, until we came to where the roof slanted and my room was under the eaves. On the way to the house we had seen a pile of tiny strawberries, the old French fraises de bois in a grocer's window, so we bought a paper coneful, and two little jars of yellow cream. And we sat in my room on the wide stone window seat, in an open gabled window that looked over the chimney pots of Paris, and ate the strawberries and cream, dipping each berry into the cream and feeding each other, and sadly watching the sun set over Paris. And we felt very triste and very young and helpless, because we could not do what we wanted to do—be happy together with no money and no fathers to worry us.

"I wonder if you really did love me when we were in Paris," Anne later wrote to Langston, suggesting that he might have tried harder to prevent her return to London. Nonetheless, the love story of wild strawberries and cream captures everything about the painful part of love, the anticipation of an unknown future. Pomme has been waiting for so long, impatient with having to be patient, and so, as an homage to Hughes for his enchanting tale, she will serve tiny wild strawberries in champagne, one glass each, as the evening begins.

Colette would never forgive a protégé who omitted cheese from the menu, a food that she said makes guests smile in true gratitude. Colette entered a cheese shop as though on an urgent mission, prodded and poked and sensed the cheeses, admired them "bound in their gilded leather, lying mysteriously beneath thick coats of lichen." Shall Pomme choose the crème à fromage that Chéri loved so well at Léa's table? The Camembert or the Saint-Florentin that Colette adored in her childhood? Pomme selects a wedge of soft cheese from Colette's native Burgundy, the pungent and spicy Soumaintrain, to serve with a warm loaf of crusty bread and a fresh garden salad, the salad presented in a bowl carved from a single piece of root from an olive tree, unwashed between uses, but rubbed clean so that the oil has impregnated the wood.

POMME'S MEAL FOR JEREMY

Champagne with Wild Strawberries
Truffles à la Colette served with a Burgundy Wine
Grilled Spring Chicken[2]
Tomates de Treille Muscate[3]
Garden Salad
Soumaintrain
Melted Chocolate with Black Cherries

"What if, after all this, he refuses me?" Pomme worries. "Shall I find the emptiness of my room, despite the scent of chocolate and berries, repressive and lonely? Will I then blame Colette, whose expertise in matters of the senses and the heart perhaps filled the evening with a surfeit of feeling, overwhelming Jeremy in a choking cloud of cloying sweetness?"

But no, this is how the evening will go. Pomme and her lover will sit by the fire, carefully melting thick slabs of dark chocolate made heady by a splash of cognac. They will dip black cherries into the dark chocolate, astonished by the burst of the fruit's complicated sweetness behind the warm chocolate shell. "Sweet things belong in a man's mouth," Jeremy will say. And then he will kiss her, finally. "Oh these quiet ones have the very devil in them," her friend Colette will say to herself as she slips softly away.

---

1. POLENTA
From *The Food of Italy,* Waverly Root, 1971

Toss a fistful of cornmeal into violently boiling salted water, stir it more or less constantly for an hour, and you have polenta. If you use a quarter more water than the normal proportion (normal is a quart of water per each cup of cornmeal,) the result is polentina, a thin gruel eaten with milk and, if you like, sugar, for breakfast, like oatmeal. It is clearly not a sophisticated dish, though there are degrees of refinement, depending . . . above all on the intuition of the cook, which determines whether it emerges from the pot sulky and soggy, or light and, after drying, flaky.

2. GRILLED SPRING CHICKEN
Adapted from *Summer Cooking,* Elizabeth David, 1955

1 spring chicken weighing about 1½ pounds, split in quarters
1 lemon
salt
ground black pepper
fresh herbs—thyme or tarragon or marjoram
olive oil
melted butter

Squeeze lemon over chicken. Season with black pepper, strew fresh herbs over the quarters, and rub with olive oil. Let the chicken sit for 1 hour.

Heat the broiler and place the chicken, skin side up, on a wire grid over a pan. Pour a little melted butter over the chicken. Let the skin brown, which will take about 5 minutes, then turn the chicken over and baste again with melted butter and broil another 5 minutes. Move the chicken into the pan, a little further from the heat, and turn the chicken again, sprinkle with coarse salt, baste with more melted butter and broil for 4 minutes. Then turn the chicken and repeat, by salting and basting and broiling for another 4 minutes or until the chicken is done, which you can tell by the golden brown skin and by cutting between the thigh and leg to see if the juices run clear. If the juice runs bloody, return to a lower heat for a few minutes.

James Beard wrote that a bearnaise sauce with tarragon accompanied the best grilled chicken that he'd ever tasted. Tarragon grew well in Colette's garden. Alternately, a Provençale method of flavoring grilled chicken calls for rubbing the chicken with rosemary halfway through cooking.

3 . TOMATES DE TREILLE MUSCATE

Select a deep red tomato. Homegrown tomatoes are the best. Avoid tomatoes that are kept in refrigerated sections in the supermarket, as the cold temperature has destroyed their flavor.

Cut the tomato into thin slices and sprinkle them lightly with olive oil and salt. Strew chopped basil leaves over them. Chopped parsley—the kind with the flat leaf—or, better yet, cilantro may be used instead.

If you prefer to serve the tomatoes in a Provençale manner, do as Waverly Root suggests in *The Food of France*. Chop and sauté tomatoes in olive oil and plenty of garlic, and sprinkle with parsley.

In *A Book of Mediterranean Food,* Elizabeth David says that perfect tomatoes Provençale should be slightly blackened on top. Cut the tomatoes in half and make small incisions crosswise in the pulp and in these rub salt, pepper, and crushed garlic. Spread each half tomato with chopped parsley, pressing it into the surface. Pour a few drops of olive oil on each half and cook under a broiler or in a hot oven.

CHAPTER TWO

Culinary Ambition

A LITERARY FEAST PLANNED BY TWO
CHEFS, ONE OF THEM POMME'S FATHER,
HENRI BOUQUIN

1 May

Henri Bouquin
Chef de Partie
The Savoy Grill
The Savoy Hotel
London

Cher Henri,

The grand opportunity of my career lies before me, the chance to elevate myself to the position of executive chef, that coveted spot for which I have worked so hard to knock out my chief competitor, the rôtisseur Michel Horsdegrasse. You'll no doubt remember him as the pock-faced provincial who once created that peculiar pot-au-feu, inspired, he said, by the Berbers of Maroc. Unhappily, this opportunity compromises my integrity by forcing me to acknowledge, even to embrace, the culinary example set by our most unfortunate colleagues. I am talking about the English. I can't fathom how you've lived there all these years among people who think that their heavy meat pies and boiled dishes constitute a national cuisine. Naturally, as a master chef of the highest order, whose subtle sauces still make my eyes tear at the memory, you will understand my dilemma, and I would be most grateful for any advice you can offer. Here, then, are my troubles in full.

Robert, the boss's son, has accepted an assignment to prepare a menu for one of L'Académie Goncourt's monthly literary luncheons. If L'Académie likes our approach, then they may bring all of their business here, a minimum commitment of twelve luncheons a year, not to mention occasional impromptu gatherings, as the members of the academy seek the annual winner of the Prix Goncourt. If Robert wins the business, then his father will hand him the restaurant and Robert will promote me to executive chef. Our Chef Daugnin is firmly entrenched in some kind of madness, and when the wine stocks are strangely depleted, I know the missing bottles of Château Latour have disappeared down his gullet. Daugnin is an old family favorite. Until Robert has charge of the restaurant, he can do nothing to rid us of him.

Robert thinks we should salute L'Académie Goncourt with a meal inspired entirely by the great writers in history. Bah! Why should I find my inspiration from writers? Writers should stick to writing, cooks to cooking. We'll have writers and their fans in here all the time, trying to catch glimpses of the members of L'Académie, lingering for hours over one drink and the cheapest plate on the menu. But L'Académie is well endowed, so I must swallow my bile and get down to the business at hand.

I hardly know where to begin. What do I know of literature? Robert is reading our own authors and has assigned me to seek inspiration from English writers. I hope that you can help me. I have little time to spare. I look forward to hearing your advice, *mon ami,* at the earliest moment.

In my haste, I almost forgot to ask after you and your family. Is your wife happy? How is Pomme? I am sure she has become quite a beauty, if she takes after Geneviève at all. Is she following your example in the kitchen, as you desired? I remember years ago how she cried when she held my hand and noticed that two of my fingers are missing. I told the dear child about my old accident with the cleaver and explained that I no longer felt any pain. To cheer her, I told her about Grimod de la Reynière, the gourmand who sheathed his false wooden hand in a glove and rested it on a burning stovetop, inviting unsuspecting others to test the heat of the stove with their own hands, burning them in a nasty surprise. The story made Pomme cry all the more. She made me promise never to do such a thing to her. If she is as sensitive in the kitchen, she has become, no doubt, a fine cook.

Please, let me hear from you as soon as possible.

Your friend,
Étienne Sansigne
PARIS

7 May

M. Étienne Sansigne
Chez Robert
Paris

Cher Sansigne,

What a surprise. I rarely receive such entertaining correspondence, but please, next time tell me more news of Paris. Here I live among people who talk of two things—whether the cellar has sufficient Veuve Cliquot for the party tomorrow (and there is *always* a party tomorrow night) and whether the English will ever stop cramming cakes into their mouths at teatime, spoiling their appetites for our marvelous dinners. But otherwise everyone here amuses me and my position is a happy one. Our chef, Virloguez, although he is a burly-looking fellow with baggy eyes, is nothing if not fair. And his elaborate creations—new desserts for every special celebration—remain the envy of every other fine London hotel. Another great source of pleasure is Mademoiselle Olivia, the patron's daughter, who brings a certain frisson to life in the kitchen. These Englishwomen, Sansigne, *écoutes,* you must try them sometime.

But your problem is no problem at all. It is, as you say, the challenge of your career, the opportunity to demonstrate your technical prowess and the height of your imagination. Do not feel so overwhelmed. After all, you have already done the right thing, which is to write to me.

First, I showed your letter to Geneviève, who is bored and lonely (still, after all the time we have lived in England), and she instantly set herself on the trail of literary inspiration. You have given her something to occupy her time and for providing that distraction, cher Sansigne, I am grateful. She goes to the library tomorrow on your behalf. We both yearn for the taste of the pâté de foie gras that the Charcuterie in rue de Clerc prepares so well. Do you think you might send us some? (Thank God neither Geneviève nor Olivia is taking part in this diet craze that has all the Englishwomen slimming down.) Although she frequently travels to Paris, Pomme has never tasted that particular pâté, and I would like her to have that pleasure. These days she no longer lives at home, which is just as well. She has become unusually moody about a musician, a man named Jeremy, whom I don't much care for. He possesses an undeniably powerful presence, but he is cool and aloof, typical of the English. He is older than Pomme—she won't tell me his age—a tall man with a bit of a belly. Nothing I could say to Pomme about Jeremy will make much difference. We have spoiled her and she is used to getting her way. She has indeed grown into a beauty, with her mother's Creole looks and a serious air of concentration. She spends much time with me in the kitchen and carries with her always the sweet scent of something pleasant bubbling on the stove.

Pomme suggests that you look to the culinary legacy of the French men of letters who happen also to be fat. Alexandre Dumas *père* comes to mind, as does Honoré de Balzac. I remember a delicious afternoon long ago making love to one of the waitresses—was it Simone or Michelle?—under his statue's great shadow in the gardens of the Musée Rodin. Tell me about *everything* you discover for your meal. I am pleased for you.

I suggest also that you locate the descendants of M. César Ritz, who returned to Paris after opening the Savoy. They may have some good stories for you about the writers who frequented the hotel.

I leave you now. I am eagerly awaiting the arrival of O. down the kitchen stairs.

Your friend,
Henri
THE SAVOY

15 May

M. Henri Bouquin
Chef de Partie
The Savoy Hotel
London

Cher Henri,

You don't know how happy I was to receive your letter and your inspired advice. I am sending you 500 grams of the Charcuterie's finest foie gras. Your family will be well fortified in your efforts on my behalf.

Henri, you never change. How do you find the time to make a magnificent impression in the dining rooms of the Savoy and keep Geneviève distracted while you make love to your mistress? As for me, after I have finished the last service, I am bone-tired and want nothing more than to retire to my bed alone.

I too have a memory of Balzac, although not so engaging a one as yours. Once I shopped for coffee beans at a shop in the rue de l'Université in Saint-Germain and noticed a portrait of Balzac on the wall. The proprietor explained that the writer used to buy coffee from his great-grandfather and that he always carried a coffee grinder wherever he went, rarely allowing others to prepare the drink for him. (Robert would not stand for that here, I'm afraid, priding himself as he does on his own method of infusion.) We will begin to practice the blend of coffee Balzac favored—Bourbon, Martinique, and Mocha. He poured streams of coffee down his throat. His doctor suspected that Balzac's abuse of coffee and late-night work habits aggravated his heart condition and caused his death. Perhaps all those Goncourt writers, like Balzac, will begin to hallucinate from excess coffee in the middle of the night, their own characters speaking back to them from the page, and, if we're lucky, they'll die and leave us poor cooks alone.

I told Robert to look up the words of the fat men, as Pomme suggested, telling him to narrow his search by consulting Balzac and Dumas. At first Robert thought I was being sarcastic, and I admit that my tone was perhaps a little bitter as we'd had a busy day, but he returned from the library with much good information. Robert discovered that Balzac rewarded himself for work well done by pounding sardines with butter to concoct a kind of pâté inspired, Balzac said, by the Rillettes de Tours. I don't understand that remark because, as you know, rillettes are made from lean pork that has been shredded and cooked for many hours in good leaf lard. The rillettes from Tours have a particularly fine texture, being made of meat from the neck of the hog with a careful blend of fat and lean pieces.

Nevertheless, I have spent the idle afternoon hour developing the ideal recipe, which I think can be served at L'Académie's dinner as an hors d'oeuvre.

SARDINE PÂTÉ AFTER THE RILLETTES DE TOURS DE BALZAC
Adapted from *An Omelette and a Glass of Wine,* Elizabeth David, 1985

Drain and debone sardines. Depending on their size, for each sardine use ½–1 tablespoon of butter and mash together well. Season with a few drops of lemon juice and pepper. Chill. Serve with bread or toast.

I located the family of M. César Ritz. His aged son granted me some time, and I brought along some of the sardine pâté to give him an idea of what I'm trying to accomplish. He became misty-eyed as he spoke of his father—admittedly he also choked on the pâté—and how an American writer named Samuel Clemens once complained of stomach trouble to César, who soothed him with a baked apple, toast, and a draught bitter. Somehow these toothless foods strike me as unsuitable for my meal. After hunting through some old boxes, Ritz dug up an old menu that shows Clemens himself dressed in white mustachios and holding a frog on a leash. What do you think that means? Should I serve frog's legs at the Goncourt dinner? While the visit with Ritz was of historical interest, he didn't help my immediate needs.

I await news of Geneviève's inspiration. Is she looking at the records of fat Englishmen, Pomme's line of inquiry that proved so fruitful on this side of the Channel?

If Pomme's romantic choice does not please you, why don't you send her here? Have Paris take her mind off the musician. I would be happy to let her use my spare room.

Your friend,
Étienne

21 May

M. Étienne Sansigne
Chez Robert
Paris

Cher Sansigne,

What a party we had here last night. A famous English actor and his usual hangers-on came to dine on my bouillabaisse laced with extra garlic. Even as I was basking in the joy of public appreciation (although the whole time I naturally pretended to a certain nonchalance), I plotted on your behalf. The group started to argue about English food. One of them talked about Virginia Woolf, an English writer they're *always* going on about in this country. "Did you know she wrote about sausage and haddock just before she died and how she tried to get a firmer grip on them by writing them down?" this woman declared over her second helping of soup. "Sausage and haddock. And within three weeks she drowned herself. Now what does *that* say about British food, then? And her poor housekeeper never got over the shock of seeing Virginia come home dripping wet one day and then disappear the next, as though she had tried to drown herself but had failed the first time."

The woman turned out to be a writer who has written a book about Woolf. When the party invited me to the table to congratulate me on my bouillabaisse, I boldly confessed to Madame my profound interest in her subject. She was pleased to talk to me and lucky for you, too. She sold me a copy of her book— she happened to have one with her—and I think you'll find something useful in it. It's called *Recollections of Virginia Woolf by Her Contemporaries.*

I have advised Pomme to visit you. She seemed unenthusiastic about leaving Jeremy at what she calls the crucial turning point in their friendship. But she mentioned that she's writing an article for a new culinary magazine about the old English coffeehouses and French cafés that requires her to go to Paris. I reminded her that if she wants to establish a name for herself in our business, she ought to work for a spell in a Parisian restaurant. I'm hoping she'll visit you and return with her old happy smile.

I am running into some expenses in acquiring this information for you. I would love to send Geneviève to the library in taxis instead of buses. And that woman charged me £20 for her book! *Incroyable!*

Amitiés,
Henri

4 June

M. Henri Bouquin
The Savoy Hotel
London

Dear Henri,

I am forever in your debt. I have good news and feel confident that I will soon be chef in these kitchens. Thank you for the book, which includes an interview with the woman who cooked and kept house for Madame Woolf, a fussy employer who often worked in her own kitchen. Mme. Woolf talked to herself in her bath, reading her own lines out loud, and they echoed in the kitchen below, a source of worry to the cook, who sounds like a simple country soul in that good-natured way the rural English possess.

Henri, can you imagine entering into the service of someone who insists on teaching you how to cook? I could not abide such a situation, especially in an English household. Mme. Woolf showed the cook how to bake a kind of bread called cottage loaf, a very passable bread that resembles a brioche in appearance and a rough, wholesome country bread in texture. I feel sure the cottage loaf will please the members of L'Académie Goncourt, and, for your amusement, I share the recipe. The cook's name was Mrs. Louie Mayer and this is her story:

She could make beautiful bread. I was surprised how complicated the process was and how accurately Mrs. Woolf carried it out. She showed me how to make the dough with the right quantities of yeast and flour, and then how to knead it. She returned three or four times during the morning to knead it again. Finally, she made the dough into the shape of a cottage loaf and baked it at just the right temperature. I would say that Mrs. Woolf was not a practical person—for instance, she could not sew or knit or drive a car—but this was a job needing practical skill which she was able to do well every time. It took me many weeks to be as good as Mrs. Woolf at making bread, but I went to great lengths practising and in the end, I think, I beat her at it.

However, the Woolfs never permitted Louie to make coffee, which Mr. Woolf prepared himself at 8 o'clock every morning. They also enjoyed game meats, like pheasant and grouse, and had an English sweet tooth for creamy puddings.

VIRGINIA WOOLF'S COTTAGE LOAVES
Adapted from *English Bread and Yeast Cookery,* Elizabeth David, 1980

5½ cups flour
½ cup whole-wheat flour
½ ounce yeast (two ¼-ounce packets of dry yeast)
1 tablespoon salt
1½–2 cups water

Mix the yeast with ½ cup very warm water and let stand.
Mix flour and salt with 1 cup water. Blend. Add yeast mixture and blend well. The dough should be fairly stiff.

Turn out onto floured surface and knead for 5 minutes or until the dough springs back when poked and the surface starts to blister. Turn dough into a greased bowl and let rise until double in bulk for one hour.

After the first rising, knead the dough for a few minutes. Divide the dough into two, one piece twice the size of the other. The larger piece is the bottom of the bread, the smaller is the topknot.

Roll each piece into a ball, turning the folds of the bottom piece under, and those of the top piece upward. Cover them to prevent the formation of a skin on the dough and let them rise separately.

After 45 minutes, assemble the loaves. (Too much proving will cause the loaf to collapse.) Flatten the top of the bottom (larger) loaf and make a cross-shaped cut about 1½ inches across in the center. Flatten the base of the top piece and perch it on the bottom piece. The flattening is critical. Without it, the bottom loaf will collapse under the weight of the topknot and the two pieces will merge while baking.

With two fingers, firmly plunge a hole through the top of the smaller loaf through its center and into the heart of the bottom loaf. This technique is called bashing and holds the two loaves together.

Place the bread on a greased and floured baking sheet. Cover it and let it rest for 10 minutes. If the dough looks slack or on the verge of collapse, put in the oven straight away.

Set the oven at 450°F just before you put the bread in the oven on the lowest rack. With gas ovens, you may want to let the oven heat for 5 minutes before placing loaf inside to prevent burning. If you have a hot oven, you may want to reduce the heat to 400°F after 15 minutes and place another baking pan on the floor of the oven to prevent burning.

After 30 minutes of baking cover the bread with a bowl to prevent the crust from becoming too hard. Toward the end of baking, remove the cover to release the steam and for the bread's final browning. The bread will take about 40 minutes to bake. The bread is done when rapping on the top and bottom of the loaf produces a hollow sound.

The bread has a moist, flavorful crumb. You must swear on your life and mine, Henri, that you will never tell a soul that I have taken cooking instruction from Englishwomen. Even so, I am relieved to have bread to serve with the sardine pâté and a cheese.

In the meantime, Robert and I have been reading Dumas's cookbook, although some of his ideas are, shall we say, a little writerly. As far as I can tell from *Grand Dictionnaire de Cuisine,* Dumas treated cooking as another form of entertainment. When he invited friends to dinner, they spent hours with him in the kitchen, cooking, singing, and talking. I myself can't approve of that kind of distracting activity. However, he suits my purpose and has an impressive sort of passion about food.

Dumas's friends told him that he had the skill of an artist in the kitchen. (They probably just wanted to flatter their way into a guaranteed place at the next free meal chez Dumas.) Robert found a letter, which I will share with you. This is from a friend of his, one of his claqueurs:

> Dumas had a faculty of invention, a gift for fantasy, a bold-
> ness in mixing ingredients and the memory of a host of
> recipes which he had learned during his travels. The bluster-
> ing, boisterous genius as easily dominated the kitchen as he
> did the literary world of the time. His cooking was energy
> and bustle personified. Meat and butter were mingled with
> fine wines in the saucepans, half a dozen sauces were being
> watched in the bain-marie, and all the while he was cracking
> jokes and laughing at most of them loudly himself.

(Henri, don't you think six sauces a little excessive for an informal meal with friends? What could he have been making?)

> Then suddenly, without the slightest warning, he would utter a melodramatic scream and rush out of the kitchen to his study. He had remembered the final denouement of a scene he had left unfinished. He would reinstate himself at his writing-table and take up the thread of the story as if no interruption whatever had occurred. Many a dish that de-lighted his guests was cooked in this extraordinary fashion, between two thrilling chapters, and the wonderful part about his culinary work was that the very dishes and ingredi-ents seemed in some unaccountable way to accommodate themselves to his casual and erratic manner. What would have been utterly ruined under any other chef seemed to succeed even extra well under his neglect.

Henri, I am confounded by the behavior of this man. How could he leave six sauces unattended on the stove while everyone else stood around in dumb amazement? Although, in one way, he reminds me of you, Henri. I picture you dashing between your wife and your mistress and then suddenly remembering your soufflé in the oven.

I stayed up two nights late to finish Dumas's dictionary and his essays on food—more than 1,500 pages of reading!—and have opted for a pasta course. (I didn't think L'Académie would enjoy his original method of cooking hare based on an Arab lamb dish. He stuffed the hare with herbs and hung it for two days until the stink of rot set in, then he cooked the beast still in its coat.) Here is his recipe for noodles, which I'll toss with butter, equal amounts of grated gruyère and Parmesan, and perhaps a little smoked ham, as Dumas suggests.

NOUILLES DE DUMAS

Adapted from *Grand Dictionnaire de Cuisine,* Alexandre Dumas,
1873

A pasta of German origin. When you want to make noodles instead of buying them readymade, take a half-liter of flour and four or five egg yolks, a little salt and a little water; mix well to make a firm dough and roll out to a thickness of five millimeters; cut the dough into strips and sprinkle with flour to prevent the strands from sticking to each other. Throw the pasta into bouillon that has been brought to the boil and let the noodles cook for a quarter of an hour, adding a spoonful of gravy or caramel or saffron for coloring. (If you think that the noodles will not dissolve while cooking, then use whole eggs instead of egg yolks.)

The recipe is a good one.

I caught our Chef Daugnin selling egg whites to the pastry shop after making hollandaise sauce. He has also been filching portions of the glaze de viande to sell to the charcuterie. I have brought his crimes to the attention of Robert, whose father still refuses to do anything about Daugnin's abuses of my kitchen. Clearly, my only hope for advancement is to win the Goncourt business.

We are getting there, my friend. Tell me more. I have enclosed some cash to cover your expenses on my behalf. Tell Pomme that I can easily find her a good position in our kitchen if she wants to take an apprenticeship here.

Étienne

10 June

M. Étienne Sansigne
Chez Robert
Paris

Dear Sansigne,

Yesterday the London branch of the Dickens Society dined here. Olivia, herself a member of the Ladies' Literary Society, assures me that the English writer who should be the greatest source of inspiration is Charles Dickens, as he writes so tenderly of starving children and, unlike most Englishmen, senses the importance of good food. When Olivia reads his novels, she cannot help but cry. She is a tender thing, Sansigne, and I bask in her affection.

Virloguez has a special champagne punch prepared for the evening based on Dickens's own recipe provided to us by the secretary of the Society. I have copied the recipe for you. By the way, any chance that you might send more foie gras? I consumed your first shipment in a delighted, gluttonous frenzy. Olivia had never tried such fine pâté, and we became carried away. Now I have none left to share with Geneviève or Pomme. A thousand pardons, cher Sansigne, for putting you to the trouble. But the pâté was delicious and made me feel for a moment as though I were back in Paris.

CHARLES DICKENS'S CHAMPAGNE CUP
Adapted from *Harper's Magazine,* May 1922

Put into a large jug 4 good lumps of sugar and the thin rind of a lemon. Cover up and stir, as above. Add a bottle of champagne, and a good tumbler and a half of sherry. Stir well. Then fill up with ice. If there be any borage, put in a good handful, as you would put a nosegay into water. Stir up well before serving.

Do not prepare the cup more than a quarter of an hour before serving, and stir before pouring.

An easy drink that should score you some easy points, friend.

Thank you for the additional research funds. While I admit to enjoying my well-placed position at the Savoy, the compensation is not quite what I desire. If I could move up the ranks myself, well, that would be another story. I am sometimes discouraged when one of my colleagues rushes back breathless from his holidays in Gex where he has dreamed up another spectacular recipe like Neige au Cliquot—a sorbet made with cream and only the 1906 vintage of the widow—or crayfish with foie gras. He thinks himself the direct successor to Virloguez. We all have our ambition, my friend.

Geneviève admitted to me that on her last trip to the library she became distracted and started reading old diaries. You should thank God for her short attention span because in one of them she came across a comment about Grasmere gingerbread that an English writer, William Wordsworth, enjoyed. The gingerbread is somewhat dry and crumbly. I hope the recipe suits L'Académie.

GRASMERE GINGERBREAD
Adapted from *The Observer Guide to British Cookery,* Jane Grigson, 1984

8 ounces white flour or fine oatmeal or ¼ pound of each

4 ounces brown sugar

2 teaspoons ginger

¼ teaspoon baking powder

8 ounces butter, melted

Mix dry ingredients together. Add melted butter to bind the dry ingredients into a dough. Line a pan with parchment paper, and spread the mixture over it in a ¼-inch layer. Bake until golden brown at 350°F for 30 to 35 minutes. Cut into oblong pieces, but leave to cool in the pan.

According to the librarian, the woman who ran the household—Dorothy, I think her name was—would have likely used finely ground oatmeal, as white flour was then a luxury.

Geneviève has become infatuated with the idea of becoming my culinary muse. I think I had better pay her a little more attention for a while. Women need occasional soft touches you know, Sansigne, to keep them on your side and in a state of surrender. They want only the chance to show how much they love you. A break from Olivia will freshen the affair once I decide to see her again. I have managed, naturally, to keep our liaison secret from her father, who would let me go if he discovered that I have stolen his daughter's affections. I also keep her from Pomme. They are the same age, and Olivia may not be so discreet as I would like.

Olivia suggested that you look at the works of two seventeenth-century English diarists she had to study in school. They are John Evelyn and Samuel Pepys. She thinks there might be something in them for you. I look forward to hearing of your progress.

Henri

16 June

Mr. Henri Bouquin
The Savoy Hotel
Paris

Cher Henri,

Thank you for the information on the gingerbread. I had never heard of Wordsworth, but the recipe will suit.

However, your lead from Olivia on Monsieur Pepys was a false one. I finally managed with extreme difficulty to locate a translation of his work. Oh là là, Henri, he wrote volumes upon volumes in very difficult language. After many hours of investigation, all I could come up with were a few remarks about trying tea and coffee and an endless procession of pies but no recipes anywhere. He mentioned burying a cask of wine and a wheel of parmezan cheese in his garden to save them from the approaching flames of the Great Fire of London. Really, what should I serve, smoked parmezan cheese? Olivia should be more certain of her facts.

Ha! I think you will agree that Olivia has wasted much of my precious time. However, I am prepared to forgive her because the other fellow, John Evelyn, had much to say about salads. He grew herbs and fresh vegetables and wrote endlessly about them, and developed an aromatic salad dressing that I plan to use.

SALLET DRESSING
Adapted from *Acetaria,* John Evelyn, 1699

The Oyl be smooth, light, and pleasant upon the Tongue; fit to allay the tartness of the Vinegar, and other Acids, yet gently to warm where it passes; 'tis incredible how small a quantity of Oyl is sufficient, to inbue a very plentiful assembly of Sallet-Herbs.

That the Vinegar be of the best Wine Vinegar, whether Distill'd, or otherwise Aromatiz'd and impregnated with the Infusion of Clove-gilly-flowers, Elder, Roses, Rosemary, Nasturtium.

Let it suffice that our Sallet-Salt be of the best ordinary Bay-Salt, clean, bright, dry, and without clamminess.

Of Sugar (by some call'd Indian-Salt) as it is rarely us'd in Sallet, it should be of the best refined, white, hard, close, yet light and sweet as the Madera's: Nourishing, preserving, cleansing, delighting the Taste, and preferable to Honey for most uses.

Note, That both this, Salt, and Vinegar, are to be proportion'd to the Constitution, as well as what is said of the Plants themselves. The one for cold, the other for hot stomachs.

That the Mustard (another noble Ingredient) be of the best Tewksbury; or else compos'd of the soundest and weightiest Yorkshire Seed temper'd to the consistence of a Pap with Vinegar, in which shavings of the Horse-Radish have been steep'd: Then cutting an Onion, and putting it into a small Earthen Gally-Pot, or some thick Glass of that shape; pour the Mustard over it, and close it very well with a Cork. There be, who preserve the Flower and Dust of the bruised Seed in a well-stopp'd Glass, to temper, and have it fresh when they please.

That the Pepper (white or black) be not bruis'd to too small a Dust; which, as we caution'd, is very prejudicial.

Of other Strewings and Aromatizers, which may likewise be admitted to inrich our Sallet, we have already spoken, where we mention Orange and Limon-peel; to which may also be added, Jamaica-Pepper, Juniper-berries, etc. as of singular Vertue.

Seventhly, That there be the Yolks of fresh and new-laid Eggs, boil'd moderately hard, to be mingl'd and mash'd with the Mustard, Oyl, and Vinegar; and part to cut into quarters, and eat with the Herbs.

I have depleted nearly all my savings on this project. Taxi fares have just gone up again, and I no longer have any choice but to walk to the market I prefer across the city. But this has turned out to be fortuitous. On my way I stopped into a fromagerie, and there I discovered the dish to serve as an entrée, a recipe of one of our own writers who understood in her very soul the mysteries and art of cuisine. I won't burden you with these details.

Your friend,
Étienne

25 June

Cher Sansigne,

Olivia finished school at sixteen and made an honest mistake in sending you to Pepys. In any case, you did get the salad recipe out of her, so don't be too hard on one who has, after all, been indispensable to your project.

But Sansigne, what is this second insult? Why did you not share with me the recipe for the entrée? You must tell me. How else can I advise you on a selection of wine to complement your meal? I had been planning to ask our wine steward for his advice, and God knows, he is not an easy man to talk to. I am offended.

Bouquin

30 June

M. Henri Bouquin
The Savoy Hotel
London

Cher Henri,

I am so sorry to have offended you. Pardon me. I am obsessed with the impending triumph of my project, so close that I nearly taste its sweet fruit and think of nothing else. Believe me, I must have been writing in an anxious haste, oblivious to anyone's feelings but my own. You are right. I should have told you the recipe for the entrée. You have been with me all along. Please accept my deepest apologies.

As I shopped in the market last week—the fromagier asked why I looked so gloomy. I explained that I had no entrée for my most important meal and only a few days left to find one. "Look no further," this man told me. "Years ago Colette shopped here. A woman most particular about her cheeses, she spent many hours in my shop, pinching and squeezing them. At first I tried to stop her, but Madame was resolute and, once I realized that she knew her cheeses, we became friendly. She gave many recipes to my wife, and I will ask her what you should do."

I paid this good man for his promise of help, and he told me to return the next day. Henri, he has saved my life, and I have resolved to read Colette's books at the first opportunity. He gave me an unusual recipe, an unorthodox way to prepare rascasse, that spiny fish which until now I thought should be used only in bouil-labaisse. I have tried this dish, which Colette once enjoyed at an auberge, a meal served under the trees in the summertime, a superb meal, a true salute to Provençale cuisine, the fish gently enhancing the other flavors.

LE POISSON DE COLETTE
Adapted from *La Treille Muscate,* Colette, 1932

You have set a fire with branches of laurel, almond, pine still seeping golden drops of resin, and the flame burns steady and low. You have at hand a beautiful piece of Mediterranean fish, gutted and cleaned, a monstrous rascasse with the throat of a dragon. You do not forget to rub a morsel of lard along the fish.

Prepare the herbs which you have tied together—perhaps sprigs of laurel, mint, pebreda, thyme, rosemary, sage—by soaking them in a pot filled with the best olive oil mixed with wine vinegar. Only a sweet red vinegar will do. Don't be naive and think we will skip over the garlic. It should be crushed until it reaches a consistency of cream and it will enrich the dressing. Salt, a little, pepper, just enough.

The fish, consecrated with the sauce, is grilled over flames that are little more than embers and a light and translucent smoke brings you the scent of the burning soul of the forest. The grilling is a matter of experience and divination. If you are not capable of a little bit of sorcery then it is not worth your while to get mixed up in the cooking. The one who grills it knows exactly how long is required.

When it is done, the fish is firm, dressed in a skin that cracks, peels away and delivers a white flesh, in which the taste is reminiscent of the sea. The resinous night descends, a lamp burning low on the table reveals the garnet of the red wine that fills your glass. Remember, with a drink of thanks, this happy moment.

Au revoir, my friend. I am delirious with my discovery. The next time we talk I shall be running this place, and I could not have done it without you.

Étienne

5 July

To: Chef Virloguez
From: Henri Bouquin
Re: A proposal for the twenty-fifth anniversary of
   The Ladies' Literary Society at the Savoy Hotel

Forgive my presumption, but the muses of literature as well as those
who inspired our own great founding chef, Monsieur Auguste
Escoffier, compel me to put forward this proposal. Consumed as I
am by thoughts of this meal—the twenty-fifth anniversary of the
Ladies Literary Society—I have taken the liberty to set down my
ideas, hoping that you will decide to serve a morsel or two. The
recipes pay tribute to some of the world's greatest writers. As the
Society is currently reading Dumas's *The Count of Monte Cristo,*
the ladies should be well entertained by eating food that he inspired. The menu lends itself to the kind of graphic presentation for
which the Savoy is renowned.

A LITERARY FEAST ON THE
OCCASION OF THE 25TH ANNIVERSARY OF
THE LADIES' LITERARY SOCIETY

Sallet and Dressing after John Evelyn
Virginia Woolf's Cottage Loaves
Sardine Pâté de Balzac
Poisson de Méditerrané de Colette
Nouilles de Dumas
Gingerbread after Dorothy Wordsworth
Champagne Cup after Charles Dickens
Smoked Parmezan Cheese after Pepys
Café de Balzac

I hope you will consider my humble suggestions.

5 July

M. Henri Bouquin
The Savoy Hotel
London

Cher Henri,

I am desolate. All is lost. We had the most extraordinary disaster
that renders my work completely lost. The day started as usual—an
early tour of the market and then to the kitchen. I checked the
inventory to see if any more wine was missing and then waited for
the news from L'Académie. I was daydreaming about my promotion when Robert rushed into the kitchen, his face a picture of pure
misery. I knew, as my heart and stomach sank, that the gravity of
his expression could relate only to my enterprise, and I began to feel
mightily sorry for myself.

L'Académie Goncourt declared our menu unacceptable. I have copied their rejection letter.

Cher M. Robert Perdant,

While we applaud your original approach in assembling foods of the great writers of our time, we cannot accept such a menu at one of our gatherings for several important reasons.

The recipe you submit from Alexandre Dumas père is problematic. Dumas claimed to be a great cook, but little evidence exists to support this. Had you done your research properly, you would realize why his cookbook received only cursory attention from the literary establishment when it was first published. You see, Dumas in his lifetime was accused of plagiarism (he was undeniably and inexplicably prolific), and this made us immediately suspicious about his life in the kitchen. While we personally enjoy a plate of noodles every now and then, that is beside the point.

Colette was indeed one of the great writers of L'Académie. But how can we salute one member and yet ignore all the others?

We were surprised that your roster of writers omitted references to writers of origins other than French and British. At first we felt you had committed a simple oversight, but then we decided that the omission had to be deliberate and, therefore, an obvious political statement at a time when France is helping to forge a united European community. Couldn't you have at least included an Italian or a German writer? Or a Spaniard?

Last, but perhaps most significant, we cannot embark on a relationship with people who do not understand the mission of L'Académie as established in Edmond de Goncourt's legacy. Our aim has been to encourage, along with literary merit, the spirit of independence in literature. By reducing literature to a mere menu, we feel you have belittled our purpose. We have decided to continue our relationship with the restaurant Drouant.

Sincerely,
The Secretary of L'Académie Goncourt

Well, Robert didn't take this easily. He stormed back to L'Académie to argue our position. He knew that Dumas had proved his culinary integrity, challenging those who accused him of plagiarism in the kitchen to watch him cook dinner. Before witnesses, Dumas prepared a complicated meal consisting of cabbage soup, stewed carp, ragout de mouton à la Hongroise, roast pheasant, and a salade Japonaise.

All this talk served no purpose. In his confrontation with the secretary, Robert had the distinct impression that our menu never reached the main body of L'Académie, that the entire exercise had been conducted at the whim of one individual, the secretary.

Henri, I have resigned from the restaurant as a point of honor. Robert's father has decided, after this monstrous waste of time and resources, that he should make his headquarters back in our establishment and keep a tighter watch over his son. I suspect I will have to leave Paris. The shame of this is almost too much to bear. Do you think there might be something for me at the Savoy?

Your friend,
Étienne

20 July

Cher Sansigne:

I am sorry to hear about your disaster.

Pomme has also had some bad news. Jeremy has left her for another woman and wants never to see her again. She has been going about the kitchens in a cold fury, a grim and determined look on her face. The last time she behaved like this was when a guest at the hotel flirted with her and told her that she lived a bloodless existence. I suppose he had been joking, but Pomme took his remark as a deep offense. The next time he stayed at the hotel he became ill with a mysterious case of food poisoning. I think the best thing for Pomme is to leave London as soon as possible. I have bought her ticket, and she'll arrive in Paris next week to finish her article for *Culture and Cuisine* magazine. I trust you will look after her during this delicate time. Make her take long walks through the city. Get her out of herself.

As for me, I have been promoted as a result of a special dinner I created last week. Virloguez says he wants me to organize the special banquets from now on, an honor I happily embrace. Now that the research on your project is done, I can spend more time with Olivia. Geneviève remains fond of her expeditions to the library, and I plan to have her research some special projects for me now and again. So your ideas were good, my dear Sansigne, but unfortunately misapplied. Didn't Robert ever investigate the source of the request from L'Académie? Oh well, that is where blind ambition will lead you. You must keep your eyes open for fools and users, Sansigne, they can do you in.

Unfortunately, there are no openings right now at the Savoy. However, I will let you know as soon as one becomes available.

Yours,
Henri Bouquin

CHAPTER THREE

The Company of Writers: Coffee, and the Literary Life

BY POMME BOUQUIN, *CULTURE AND CUISINE* MAGAZINE

> For the atmosphere of a proper café implies these qualities, fellowship, the satisfactions of the belly, and a certain gaiety and grace of behavior. . . . There, for a few hours at least, the deep bitter knowing that you are not worth much in this world could be laid low.
>
> —Carson McCullers
> *The Ballad of the Sad Café*

I have often stared deeply into my cup of coffee, dreaming about the history of civilization resting for the moment in my hands. Beneath the sleek surface lie vicious battles to capture new trading routes and dominate the coffee trade, sudden encounters between cultures strange to one another who fought and died for the sake of a bean, extraordinary careers of merchants and adventurers who left their women waiting at home.

If you prefer tea, you'll discover similar stories in your cup. Of the *Cutty Sark,* sailing into London, home from the South China Sea, of European and American traders who shipped opium to China to pry open its seaports, of merchants who forced their children into strategic marriages and ignored the angry tears of their daughters and sons, of smugglers who catered to those who didn't care to pay taxes on their cup of tea. If the silky taste of chocolate is your desire, know that the luxuriant drink sweetly conceals thousands of lives lost for the sake of the rich, oily cocoa bean, the story of the Spanish *conquistadores* who came to the Aztecs for gold and took chocolate too.

Coffee, tea, and chocolate also tell the story of writers. Look more keenly into your cup to find a small chapter in the history of literature kept warm in its heat, the story of the literary life surrounding the old London coffeehouses and the Paris cafés.

The Coffeehouses of London

Imagine James Farr's anxiety in 1657 as he stood before the magistrate at St. Dunstan's and listened to the Disorders and Annoys charges brought against him. "We present James Farr, barber and proprietor of the Rainbowe Coffee House on Fleet Street for making and selling of a drink called coffee, whereby in makeing the same, you annoyeth your neighbors by evil smells and for keeping of ffier for the most part nights and day, whereby your chimney and chamber hath been set on ffire, to the great danger and affrightment of your neighbors." Farr's was the second coffeehouse to open in London. Three complainants, all booksellers, had argued that his furnace would cause a fire. The association of coffee and literature had started very badly, yet the booksellers had been right to worry. Nine years later, the Great Fire of London broke out in Pudding

Lane, most likely in a bakery, and burned for five days, wrecking property in prosperous residential and business neighborhoods, destroying virtually everything between the Temple and the Tower of London. The Rainbowe Coffee House was spared.

Coffee at first seemed exotic to the English and they debated its benefits and recipes. Handbills promoting "The Vertue of the Coffee Drink, First made and publickly sold in England by Pasqua Rosee" proclaimed coffee's salutary effect on digestion, sore eyes, gout, dropsy, scurvy, spleen, hypochondriac winds, and drowsiness. A rival handbill, "A Broadside Against Coffee," mocked Rosee's extravagant claims:

> . . . And yet they tell ye that it will not burn,
> Though on the jury blisters you return;
> Whose furious heat does make the water rise,
> And still through the alembics of your eyes.
> Dread and desire, you fall to 't snap by snap,
> As hungry dogs do scalding porridge lap.
> But to cure drunkards it has got great fame;
> Posset or porridge, will 't not do the same?

While the Turkish then flavored their coffee with spices like cinnamon, cloves, and essence of ambergris, and prepared coffee by boiling the ground beans, the English had other ways, often boiling their coffee with sugar candy and sometimes even with mustard.

ELECTUARY OF COFFEE

A 1657 RECIPE

Take equal quantity of Butter and Sallet-oil, melt them well together, but not boyle them: then stir them well that they may incorporate together: then melt therewith three times as much Honey, and stir it well together: then add thereunto powder of Turkish Cophie, to make it a thick Electuary.

Another recipe called for oatmeal, Cophie, ale or wine, ginger, honey or sugar, and butter—ingredients that must have disguised rather than enhanced the taste of coffee. Butter at first seems like a greasy component of a coffee elixir, but think of the generous amount of fat contained in milk and cream taken in coffee today. Coffeehouses also served chocolate, a drink thick with the fat of roasted cocoa beans.

I remember my first sip of coffee. The seductive aroma belied its sharp and bitter flavor, and I was disappointed. Samuel Pepys wrote about first trying coffee in the late 1600s, finding it strange and bitter, but came to enjoy the taste. He frequented the coffeehouses as part of his social and professional life, paying two pennies to sit and drink all he liked. Picture yourself at a coffeehouse in 1667, listening to Pepys talk about watching the flames of the Great Fire approach and then, miraculously, burn itself out before it reached his home. As you drink coffee with him, you might order a meat pie or sherbet, or take ale, tea, or chocolate instead. If you meet Pepys at an alehouse, you might sample foods intended to provoke your thirst, like anchovies, slices of ham, cod's roe, prawns, powdered beef, toasted cheese, snapdragons, and pickled herring.

Or let's say you're a budding writer of the 1700s. You'll drop by the Chapter Coffee House, one of two thousand such establishments throughout London, where you'll improve your contacts among booksellers and publishers. You might stop off at Button's or Will's or Tom's in Great Russell Street to listen to the famous wits and writers of the day and, as Jonathan Swift declared, return home with your head filled with trash. Swift mocked the pretentiousness of the coffeehouse literary scene in *Hints Toward an Essay on Conversation:*

> And indeed, the worst Conversation I ever remember to have heard in my Life was that at Wills Coffee-house, where the Wits (as they were called) used formerly to assemble; that is to say, five or six Men, who had writ Plays, or at least Prologues, or had Share in a Miscellany, came thither, and entertained one another with their trifling Composures, in so important an Air, as if they had been the noblest Efforts of human Nature, or that the Fate of their Kingdoms depended on them; and they were usually attended with an humble Audience of young Students from the Inns of Courts, or the Universities, who, at due Distance, listened to these Oracles, and returned Home with great Contempt for their Law and Philosophy, their Heads filled with Trash, under the Name of Politeness, Criticism and Belles Lettres.

If you are lucky and manage to impress Jacob Tonson, the publisher of Milton's *Paradise Lost* and Shakespeare, he'll invite you to a meal at the Kit-Kat Club, convening at the home of Chris Kat. In return for the food and drink—the "whet"—you'll agree, as is customary, to give the publisher the right of first refusal of your work. Kat, a baker, is renowned for his Katt Pies, which resemble mince tarts and are filled with ground lamb, sugar, currants, rum, nuts, and spices.

I would love to have accompanied the writers at the coffee-houses, but they would have welcomed me only as a serving maid. Men thrived on coffee culture. Writers, artists, politicians, scientists, philosophers, gamblers, and actors gathered around steaming pots of coffee at their preferred coffeehouses, where they could find out the news of the day, talk with their friends, debate the latest political events. *The Spectator* reported on cultural and political affairs seen and overheard at the coffeehouses, noting the new fashions sported at the Rainbowe—silver garters buckled below the knee. While keeping men abreast of the latest coffeehouse trends, *The Spectator* cautioned its fair readers, restless at home, to beware the inflammatory dangers of eating chocolate and reading novels.

Joseph Addison, classical scholar, poet, member of Parliament, and contributor to *The Spectator,* visited the coffeehouses to gauge the diversity of popular opinion. When England warred with France and rumors of King Louis XIV's death reached London in the spring of 1715, Addison set out on a coffeehouse ramble. At the politically minded St. James coffeehouse, he discovered men huddled about the coffee pot who settled the matter of the King's succession in less than a quarter of an hour. Addison pressed on. At Gile's, he found French gentlemen living in exile planning their reestablishment in France. At Jenny Mann's, a young man announced that "the old prig is dead at last" and talked of storming Paris. At Will's, customers with literary inclinations wistfully imagined the marvelous elegies that the deceased great writers Boileau, Racine, and Corneille would have composed on "so eminent a patron of learning." In a Fish Street coffeehouse, a thoughtful man explained how the King's death would improve the pilchard and mackerel trade. In another, debate raged about whether the King resembled Caesar Augustus or Nero. Finally, in a Cheapside coffeehouse, news arrived that King Louis XIV had been out hunting the day before, very much alive. The report concluded Addison's ramble, which became the topic of *The Spectator* on Thursday, June 12, 1715.

Proud of his coffeehouse wanderings, Addison wrote, "I shall be ambitious to have it said of me that I have brought philosophy out of closets and libraries, schools and colleges, to dwell in clubs and assemblies, at tea-tables and coffee-houses." The man who spun verse in Latin and led Parliamentary debate saw himself, at heart, as a coffeehouse scholar.

Coffeehouses thrived through the 1700s, but in the early 1800s, the more expensive private clubs, taverns, and hotels gradually took their place. But in Paris, the cafés thrived as essential and accessible arenas for literary culture.

Romance and Ritual—Coffee and the Paris Cafés

I am grateful for uncomplicated pleasures—sipping from a steaming cup of coffee at a favorite café, watching the world, taking solace in the company of friends or strangers. But cafés have offered writers something far more crucial than simple pleasure. Café life has formed the essential part—if not the heart—of literary life. Solitude may be necessary for writers, but cafés have saved them from complete isolation, providing inexpensive and warm places to write, respite from the ardors of writing, and an excuse to defer work. Some writers, such as Balzac and Stendhal, regarded coffee almost as a drug, a way to stay awake and to stimulate creativity. Stendhal studied philosophy and drama in his Paris attic room and routinely flooded himself with coffee for the benefit of his art. "I've been drinking a demitasse of coffee every day for the past month, I didn't drink any today and I'm infinitely gayer, more on a level with other men," he wrote in his diary on May 17, 1805. "It would seem that coffee produces genius and gloominess; I've already experienced this result, which is striking in my case, several times."

I imagine a morning in the early nineteenth century when Balzac awoke with the taste of disgust in his mouth. Hopelessly behind in his novel, he would never meet his deadline. The printer would no doubt complain about the writer's difficult dense scrawl and charge a small fortune for another set of revised proofs, but he always accommodated Balzac's last-minute changes. No, that was not Balzac's concern. While he was writing through the night, putting flesh on his courtesan, a character in the prime of her passion, he had reached for the pot of coffee on the fire intending to stoke his energy for a final bout with his characters as dawn broke over Paris. Disaster. He spilled the coffee and doused the fire. Worse, after a disheartening rummage in the pantry, he discovered that he had run out of coffee. Then he knew, as he slipped into exhaustion, that he had lost precious hours as well as the will to carry on until he could buy more coffee. The courtesan faded on the page as Balzac fell into an uneasy sleep until daybreak, the moment when he could pound on a friend's door, calling him out on an expedition to buy coffee. Balzac's daytime sorties risked attracting the attention of debt collectors, but he could not work without coffee. Then he was off. No time even for a letter to his beloved Madame Hanska. She would be well entertained by his follies in a later correspondence.

"Coffee glides down into one's stomach and sets everything in motion," Balzac wrote:

> One's ideas advance in columns of route like battalions of
> the Grande Armée. Memories come up at the double bear-
> ing the standards which are to lead the troops into battle.
> The light cavalry deploys at the gallop. The artillery of logic

thunders along with its supply wagons and shells. Brilliant notions join in the combat as sharpshooters. The characters don their costumes, the paper is covered with ink, the battle has begun and ends with an outpouring of black fluid like a real battlefield enveloped in swathes of black smoke from the expended gunpowder.

Balzac's coffee campaigns required at least half a day's journey across Paris. He favored a blend of three coffee beans—Mocha from a grocer in the rue de l'Université in the Faubourg St. Germain, Martinique from the rue des Vieilles Audriettes, and Bourbon from the rue de Montblanc. Alexandre Dumas père, Balzac's contemporary, explained in his cookbook, *Grand Dictionnaire de Cuisine,* that Mocha coffee has a strong aroma and deep flavor and is usually mixed equally with Bourbon coffee. Martinique, Dumas wrote, was seldom drunk except with milk because of its bitterness. Balzac did not generally care for milk in his coffee, calling the notion ridiculous and unhealthy, although he would sometimes take café crème or espresso with steamed milk or whipped cream. Balzac's coffee earned rave reviews, this one from Léon Gozlan, a friend and later the writer's biographer who accompanied Balzac on his coffee excursions:

> After dinner we usually had coffee on the terrace: Balzac's coffee was proverbially excellent. I doubt that Voltaire's was superior. Such color! Such an aroma! He made it himself, or at least supervised its making. It was a masterly concoction, subtle, divine—like his own genius.

Let Balzac lead your next journey to Paris, as he's led mine. Don't succumb to the literary sightseeing industry that directs

English-speaking tourists to the cafés that Ernest Hemingway visited—the Café Dôme, where he drank his morning coffee until the
place filled with noisy people who wanted only to be seen; or Le
Closerie de Lilas, where he wrote much of *The Sun Also Rises,*
reading the work aloud to a friend, the writer John Dos Passos.
Don't fall for the Hemingway package deal, feeling romantically
reverent as you retrace the writer's routes, believing his version of
Paris in *A Moveable Feast,* his satisfaction about writerly rituals and
about being young and in love and in Paris. The absence of a
literary café life in twentieth-century England and the United States
makes Hemingway's story appealing—so passionate, so very
French. But what Hemingway described is merely an expatriate
version, the story of romantically reckless Americans in Paris. In
those years, Hart Crane engaged in a furniture-bashing battle with
the police at the Café Select; the self-appointed English-speaking
literati snubbed Sinclair Lewis at a café because of his commercial
success; and Henry Miller sat in his regular spot and bemoaned that
the whores of Paris were the only pure beings in a world of stinking
garbage.

No, the Hemingway thing by now is overdone, contrived.
Rather than indulge in the languid experience of waiting to be
served in a café, barely recapturing the lively spirit of Paris's literary
coffee rituals, embark instead on Balzac's trek for coffee, a grand
tour of the city, exciting in its urgency. Seek the places favored by
writers like Voltaire (who in his later years preferred a blend of
chocolate and coffee). "He thinks he's a public figure because he
goes to the theater and to the Procope," Voltaire complained about
a contemporary poet. Le Procope, among the first cafés in Paris,
opened around 1643. With a clientele that included Voltaire and
Jean-Jacques Rousseau, Le Procope had the distinction of becoming Paris's first literary café. Look for the place where the Café de

Rouen stood, the one that Stendhal abandoned after nine years of patronage when he fought with another customer. Prowl the city at night in memory of the novelist George Sand, a woman who dressed like a man in order to roam freely, who suffered great loneliness after her love affair with the writer Alfred de Musset ended. She played dominoes all night at cafés rather than staying at home by herself.

Walk the Boulevard des Italiens where the Café Riche once stood, where the Goncourt brothers sneered at other writers, jealously. "Café Riche seems to be in a way to become the camp of those men of letters who wear gloves . . . the commoners of literature dare not venture," they wrote in their journal in October 1857. "Baudelaire took supper tonight at the table next to ours. He was without a cravat, his shirt open at the throat, his head shaved, absolutely the toilette of a man ready for the guillotine. At bottom, however, the whole appearance carefully staged: his little hands washed, their nails cleaned, as tended as the hands of a woman."

Charles Baudelaire used the cafés as a stage to appall others and as a haven from his mistress Jeanne Duval, the Vénus noire of his poetry, with whom he lived a tempestuous, syphilitic, devoted love affair. Other customers at the café eavesdropped and thrilled to hear his shocking opinions. Stories circulated about how he praised the delicate taste and aroma of a child's brain and boasted that his emaciated appearance owed to a steady diet of stewed frogs. In truth, he was addicted to opium.

Cafés measured a style of life passing away. In 1860, the Goncourts complained that the Paris they knew and loved was vanishing, materially and morally, never learning that life brings constant surprise and change. "Social life is the way of a great evolution," they wrote. "I see women, children, men and their wives, families, in the cafés. The home is dying. Life threatens to become public." Life had already become public. The Goncourts themselves craved public attention and played out their private lives before strangers. Edmond, frustrated with his brother's increasingly paranoid and morose behavior, scolded him over dinner at a restaurant, and Jules burst into tears, crying, *"Ce n'est pas de ma faute!* It's not my fault!" They wept uncontrollably. Jules was going mad from syphilis.

The cafés had become a forum for celebrity, and for those who vaunted a self-styled decadence in their literature and in their lives, like the dissolute poets Rimbaud and Verlaine, cafés promoted their notoriety. Rimbaud slashed Verlaine's wrists in the Café du Rat Mort (Dead Rat Café.) In retaliation, Verlaine shot Rimbaud and served a two-year jail sentence, the performance prompting one critic to call them literary hooligans. With art mirroring life, Paris cafés appeared in fiction. Maxime seduced his stepmother in the Café Riche in Zola's *La Curée*. Frederic and Rosanette dined at Café Anglais in Flaubert's *Sentimental Education*. Balzac, known for futile attempts to rid himself of debt, wrote a scene set in Frascati's where his character, Lucien de Rubempré, gambles, desperate for funds.

One century later, the cafés served as writing studios for Jean-Paul Sartre and Simone de Beauvoir. A reference to coffee is one of many romantic observations that Beauvoir allows herself in her memoirs. She describes how she and Sartre sat together: "A cup of coffee became a kaleidoscope in which we could spend ages watching the mutable reflections of ceiling or chandelier. We invented one past for the violinist, and quite a different one for the pianist." A congenial and essential part of literary history has depended on the companionable warmth of the cafés and the rituals surrounding coffee. Simple pleasures are essential pleasures, restorative, necessary to survival.

I think of Colette in her old age, her husband, Maurice Goudeket, sitting on the edge of her bed, finding her beautiful still, the blue lamp behind her throwing strange lights through the thinning, frizzy hair. They had long stopped sleeping together, content with their ardent friendship. Occasionally, Colette received literary admirers in her room and let them gather about her to receive the secrets of how she created Claudine, a character she often described as her own double. But for breakfast, Goudeket had her to himself.

"Colette split open her croissant with a knife without ever letting a crumb fall and goodness knows how difficult that is, buttered it slowly and salted the butter," Goudeket wrote. "She took very little milk and a lot of sugar in her coffee, and—yes indeed!—she dipped her croissant in it just as does every French person and no English person who respects himself." There "really is in every author a tea-behavior or a coffee-behavior," and who knows, he went on to say, that these things don't have a significance in their work.

Only Marcel Proust, maddeningly fastidious, rivals Colette in the ritual of drinking coffee. The preparation and service of his café au lait and croissant took on a churchlike solemnity demanding the participation of his entire household and several neighborhood merchants. Proust required the Corcellet brand of coffee, bought only from the shop where the beans were roasted, and that the coffee be filtered one drop at a time. A local dairy delivered fresh milk every morning, leaving the bottles outside so that Proust wouldn't be disturbed while he slept. If Proust slept in very late, the woman who brought the milk returned at noon to exchange the bottles for fresh ones. When Proust rang for his croissant, his housekeeper Céleste entered a bedroom filled with the smoke of the fumigation powder that the writer burned to fight his asthma:

> All I could see of M. Proust was a white shirt under a thick
> sweater, and the upper part of his body propped against two

pillows. His face was hidden in the shadows and the smoke from the fumigation, completely invisible except for the eyes looking at me—and I felt rather than saw them. . . . I bowed toward the invisible face and put the saucer with the croissant down on the tray. He gave a wave of the hand, presumably to thank me, but didn't say a word. Then I left.

If coffee rituals are filled with consequence, as the lives and words of the writers suggest, then you must begin to take your morning coffee and croissant most seriously. Develop your own coffee ritual. If literary hooliganism is the reputation you desire, frequent a well-chosen café to work intently and noticeably on your manuscript. Mutter shocking things in a voice just loud enough to attract attention. You are bound to enhance your notoriety, your reputation for eccentricity, and certainly your literary stature. You want others to talk about you, your name to be in their mind and on their tongue. Bring your friends and say witty things about the latest best-selling novel in a supercilious tone. Call for your coffee and croissant. The café proprietor knows your tastes and serves you promptly, careful to avoid clanking the spoon against your cup, a mistake liable to cost him his tip. Make your displeasure known if the coffee is not warmed to the precise temperature you require. Be proud. You have entered the literary life.

But perhaps you long for the solace of an environment where you do not stand out by being alone. You yearn for the bracing warmth of strong coffee and the gregarious hum of a crowd of strangers that leaves you to tend your thoughts. Take the coffee's heat to your heart and your belly as you watch the people around you, as you watch yourself. Let the coffee ritual do for you what it has for so many writers, restore your creativity, bring you back home to yourself, soothe you.

CHAPTER FOUR

Passion Gone Sour

POMME DEVELOPS A TASTE FOR REVENGE

The story, like many love affairs, started at a dinner table and continued with headaches in many places.

—Graham Greene
Ways of Escape

Consider the moral, I pray,
Nor bring a young fellow to sorrow,
Who loves this young lady today,
And loves that young lady tomorrow.
You cannot eat breakfast all day,
Nor is it the act of a sinner,
When breakfast is taken away,
To turn your attention to dinner;
And it's not in the range of belief,
That you could hold him as a glutton,
Who, when he is tired of beef,
Determines to tackle the mutton.

—Gilbert and Sullivan
Trial by Jury

*A*lone, in Paris, Pomme imagines Colette.

So he's left you, Pomme. They do that, you know, and you are no stranger to that idea, flighty and wander-eyed yourself, quick to dart off to the next man who intrigues you with the promise of a new and wholly different adventure. Come, *chérie,* you must not think of him any longer, and don't tell me that this time is different. You are angry only because Jeremy was the one to end the affair. Now you must learn to care for yourself. Until you know how to be alone, to harness and use your passion, you are of no use to anyone.

I am wiser and have gained experience, Pomme tells herself, trying to put her anger aside as she wanders into the kitchen. She sets a saucepan of water mixed with cinnamon and cloves and orange peel on a low-burning flame, hoping that the spices' thick scent will soothe her. But freshly scorned, she is short on forgive-ness and impatient with Colette, the one who helped her seduce Jeremy in the first place. What I really need, she tells herself, is a recipe for revenge, the gift of a poisoned apple wrapped irresistibly with a note of love falsely signed by his new girlfriend. Or a fruit basket bearing the apples of Sodom, freshly plucked from their grove by the Dead Sea, beautiful to behold but bitter and filled with ashes. Pomme smiles at the thought of Jeremy's long fingers curling possessively around the fruit and his look of startled surprise when his greedy mouth suddenly fills with grit. Will he picture her face in that moment? Will that shatter his indifference? She reaches for a bright green apple, and then for a cookbook where she looks for her revenge, a meal she will prepare for him when she returns to London.

NEW ENGLAND APPLE PIE OR
A RECIPE FOR VENGEANCE
From *A Tramp Abroad,* Mark Twain, 1879

To make this excellent breakfast dish, proceed as follows: Take a sufficiency of water and a sufficiency of flour, and construct a bullet-proof dough. Work this into the form of a disk, with the edges turned up some three-fourths of an inch. Toughen and kiln-dry it a couple of days in a mild but unvarying temperature. Construct a cover for this redoubt in the same way and of the same material. Fill with stewed dried apples; aggravate with cloves, lemon-peel, and slabs of citron; add two portions of New Orleans sugar, then solder on the lid and set in a safe place till it petrifies. Serve cold at breakfast and invite your enemy.

A repulsive dish. A vicious meal. A recipe for a certain bad stomach. Yet Pomme knows New England Apple Pie is far from fatal. Besides, she has no plans ever to have breakfast with Jeremy again. She reaches for another book, Dumas's *The Count of Monte Cristo,* in which the Count plants the idea of poison in a woman's mind, making her his instrument in a terrible, deserved revenge against her husband.

THE COUNT OF MONTE CRISTO'S
RECIPE FOR A POISON TO BE
ADMINISTERED IN LEMONADE ON AN
ANGRY, HOT SUMMER'S DAY

Supposing the poison were brucine and that you took a milligram the first day, two milligrams the second day, and so on progressively. Well, at the end of ten days you would

RECKLESS APPETITES / 65

have taken a centigram; at the end of twenty days, by increasing this by another milligram, you would have taken
another three centigrams; that is to say, a dose you would
absorb without suffering inconvenience, but which would be
extremely dangerous for any other person who had not
taken the same precautions as yourself.

Pomme could find a way to meet Jeremy and then slip the
poison into the grog he loves so well. Three or four tablespoons of
sugar stirred into a glass of hot water, the juice and pulp of a lemon,
a strong splash of rum. And a little brucine to which she will inure
herself over a period of twenty days, inviting him on the twenty-first
for an evening's drink and supposed rapprochement. Pomme
cheers and begins her shopping list. Fresh lemons. Rum. Brucine,
enough for twenty-one days.

Another poison, wormwood, a leafy plant more commonly
known as absinthe, would also suffice. Pomme is well aware of
Jeremy's tendency toward gluttony, a weakness he tried unsuccess-
fully to hide. The trick will be to encourage him to develop a taste
for the drink, violently green in appearance like chartreuse and
toxic when taken in sufficient quantity. She'll pour a glass for him
and then fill his head with romantic stories of the writers and artists
who lounged at the Café Voltaire in Paris who were unable to resist
the deadly drink. "Even when made less offensive by a trickle of
sugar," one participant in the café scene noted, "absinthe still reeks
of copper, leaving on the palate a taste like a metal button slowly
sucked." And yet many drank it and became ill from it, and some
died. They did not understand the poison's causal relationship with
cortex lesions in the brain.

Pomme knows she may have trouble finding absinthe and
keeping Jeremy supplied. Easier instead to hook him on opium—

the habit of Charles Baudelaire, Samuel Taylor Coleridge, Thomas de Quincey, and Wilkie Collins—who drank opium, honey, and alcohol mixed in hot water, a blood-red elixir called laudanum. De Quincey, author of *Confessions of an English Opium Eater,* sustained himself on laudanum, rice, tea, and scraps of meat and, like Baudelaire, may have taken opium as a painkiller for recurring bouts of syphilis. His neighbor, Coleridge, drank two pints of laudanum a day for most of his life. With powerful opiate elixirs widely available, such as the one with the brand name "Black Drop," Wilkie Collins took laudanum to counter his attacks of gout. In his novel *The Moonstone,* he evoked the drug's mysterious quality, calling it the "all-powerful and all-merciful drug," glossing over its attendant symptoms of mental and physical deterioration. Constipation and nausea, loss of appetite and weight, decline in self-respect, careless habits, impaired concentration, lack of responsibility and consideration for others, and lying are the symptoms of opium addiction that insidiously invaded the bodies and minds of these men. As Coleridge fell deeper into addiction, the pleasant hallucinations of his early days evolved into visions of terror. For Baudelaire, addiction became his destroyer and his salvation. "In this world of mine," he wrote, "narrow but crammed with disgust, only one well-known object smiles upon me: the phial of laudanum. An old and terrible mistress—lavish, like all mistresses, alas, with her caresses and betrayals."

Laudanum will eventually give Jeremy strange and dreadful nightmares, like those recorded by Coleridge in 1802 in which his friends William, Mary, and Dorothy Wordsworth appear, the latter "altered in every feature, a fat, thick-limbed and rather red-haired—in short, no resemblance to her at all—" and "a frightful pale woman who, I thought, wanted to kiss me, and had the property of giving a shameful Disease by breathing in the face." Jeremy will dream of his new girlfriend as a monstrous apparition, like the three-fingered dwarf that grasped Coleridge's scrotum in the night, waking him up screaming.

Pomme turns her mind to the food she'll serve with the lethal drink. "If a waiter in a restaurant has a grudge against one, he will spit into one's food," H. L. Mencken said. She will do that too, but only for starters. More fatal methods will spoil his food and his life. The toxic oil in nutmeg will prompt hallucinations, with unpleasant side effects of headaches, nausea, and cramps. A spinach and rhubarb pie will foster kidney stones; a bounty of yellow foods rich in carotene, like carrots, eggs, and mangoes, will bring on jaundice; while an abundance of onions will provoke anemia. Pomme used to avoid onions in the meals she so lovingly prepared for Jeremy.

On the Use of Onions in Cooking
by Jonathan Swift

> For this is every cook's opinion,
> No savoury dish without an onion;
> But lest your kissing should be spoiled,
> Your onions must be thoroughly boiled.

Now that Jeremy's kisses have spoiled for Pomme, onions have become most desirable to give him sour breath to inflict on the new girlfriend.

So many possibilities—a surplus of cabbage to cause goiter, a salad dressing blended with a raw egg possibly harboring the salmonella bacteria, or a plate of marinated mushrooms on which Pomme would place a deadly toadstool, reminiscent of Katherine Mansfield's troubles with love that she complained of in her journal:

> If only one could tell true love from false love as one can tell
> mushrooms from toadstools. With mushrooms it is so sim-

ple—you salt them well, put them aside and have patience. But with love, you have no sooner lighted on anything that bears even the remotest resemblance to it than you are perfectly certain it is not only a genuine specimen, but perhaps the only genuine mushroom ungathered.

Pomme well knows that false love is as poisonous as a toadstool.

Other foods may help Pomme exact her revenge. She'll substitute hemlock leaf for parsley in a fresh garden salad sprinkled with roasted apple seeds, rich in sugar-cyanide complexes to inhibit his respiratory system. She might end the meal by serving a simple cake with a deadly lily of the valley embedded in its pretty glaze, or else an enchanted dessert like the Turkish Delight from C. S. Lewis's *The Chronicles of Narnia,* for whose sweet taste many killed themselves, mad from desire. If not the magical kind of Delight that Lewis described, then Pomme will serve an inferior version of the imported sweet, tainted with red lead to produce a brilliant vermilion color.

Although Pomme enjoys the idea of deceitful meals, she knows the foods will take too long to make their deadly effects known. Besides, Jeremy will likely balk at unusual foods, suspicious of discordant and jarring tastes, unlike the seductive feasts she has created for him in the past. She'll tell him that they're recipes she's learned during her apprenticeship in Paris, but she doubts he'll believe her. Pomme wonders, as she browses for another dish, if a simpler and more effective revenge might be one worked from behind the scenes. Jeremy is no fool, and she must be discreet. She reads Zora Neale Hurston's *Mules and Men* and finds a perfect recipe calling for a spicy gumbo that has been thickened with powdered sassafras leaf or filé:

ZORA NEALE HURSTON ON HOW
TO KILL AND HARM
A Southern folk recipe (1935)

Get bad vinegar, beef gall, filet gumbo with red pepper, and put names written across each other in bottles. Shake the bottle for nine mornings and talk and tell it what you want it to do. To kill the victim, turn it upside down and bury it breast deep, and he will die.

But then the feckless lowdown lovers in Carson McCullers's *The Ballad of the Sad Café* make clear the course of action she should take. Like them, Pomme slyly plans to prepare one of Jeremy's favorite dishes, perfectly spiced and delicately scented, to leave like a tantalizing trap, lavishly doctored with a killing dose of poison. She will play on Jeremy's sweet tooth and consults a helpful passage in Balzac's *Splendeurs et Misères des Courtesanes,* the scene from the chapter called "How Much Love Costs Old Men" in which a man eats ice cream from the restaurant Tortoni.

> At the end of supper, the guests were served with ices called plombières. As everyone knows, this kind of ice contains tiny comfits of fruit placed upon its surface and is served in small glasses. . . .

Within the evening the man died. His enemies had poisoned the pretty dessert.

Tortoni's—a restaurant frequented by Balzac, Dumas, Hugo, dandies, and Stock Exchange people pretending to be men of style—served the creamiest ice creams in Paris. Pomme looks for the recipes and considers how she might serve them most effectively.

PLOMBIÈRES

According to *Le Répertoire de la Cuisine,* plombières are composed of vanilla ice with apricot marmalade and candied fruits soaked in kirsch. *Larousse Gastronomique*'s version of the dessert, adapted as follows, is an almond-based custard.

Grind 2 cups of almonds, gradually adding ½ cup milk. Scald 5½ cups of cream, and add to almonds, and mix. Rub through a fine sieve.

Beat 1½ cups of sugar and 12 egg yolks in a large bowl, until the mixture pales and thickens.

Bring the almond milk to a boil, and whisk it into the egg and sugar mixture. Place over the heat and stir gently until the cream coats the back of a wooden spoon. Immerse the base of the saucepan in cold water to stop the cooking process and whisk until the cream has cooled. Place in an ice cream freezer.

When the mixture is partially frozen, mix in 1 cup finely chopped candied fruit that has been soaked in kirsch or rum. Add 1¾ cups whipped and chilled heavy cream and ⅔ cup cold milk. Then place in an ice cream mold and freeze.

BISCUITS TORTONI
Adapted from *Good Things,* Jane Grigson, 1971

Margaret Visser in *Much Depends on Dinner* says that Biscuits Tortoni are a frozen cream mousse with macaroons, almonds, and rum. Grigson's recipe calls for sherry.

2 cups each of heavy cream and light cream
½ cup confectioners sugar
pinch of salt
1 cup crushed macaroons
⅔ cup sherry

Beat the creams with the sugar and salt, and freeze until just firm.
Fold in crumbs and sherry. Add more sugar if necessary.

Freeze in a metal loaf tin or other pan. When ready to serve, turn
out and decorate with extra crumbs. (To turn out, wrap the tin with
a cloth soaked in hot water.)

For variation, ground almonds may be added with the crushed
macaroons.

To crown her revenge, Pomme will top the ice cream with a
handsome dollop of redcurrant jam, the one from *Madame Bovary*.
Emma Bovary's neighbor, the pharmacist Homais, excelled in preparing various conserves, vinegars, and sweet liqueurs. While
making redcurrant jam one day, Homais's servant brought tools
that had handled arsenic, a tasteless and odorless poison. The
servant's error was caught in time. Pomme could let herself into
Jeremy's house—he has forgotten to reclaim her set of his keys—to
hide a jar of festively wrapped, poisoned jam at the back of his
pantry with a fond note. Jeremy will discover it one day and think
it one last gift from her kitchen. He won't be able to resist. An acute
dose will burn his mouth and throat and hold his stomach in a vise
grip, and he'll die in a matter of hours. More gradual doses will
drain his energy, give him constipation, make his skin turn scaly.
He'll feel paralyzed and confused, and soon he will die. His greed
and the redcurrant jam will serve as Pomme's instruments of vengeance.

Pomme turns to a cookbook popular in Flaubert's day for a
recipe for redcurrant jam:

HOMAIS'S REDCURRANT JAM
Adapted from *The Household Cookery Book,*
Félix Urbain-Dubois, 1871

Choose the currants red, but not overripe; remove the berries from the stalks; weigh them, put them into an untinned copper basin; mix into them 2 pounds of sugar, to each pound of fruit; let the sugar and the fruits macerate for one hour, stirring them from time to time; set the basin on a fire, give the liquid 4 or 5 minutes ebullition, and pour it, together with the fruit, on a sieve, placed over a kitchen basin. The jelly passes limpid, and is set, as soon as it has cooled.

Pomme's rash thoughts tire her. Perhaps after all she'll simply wish on him the torture of unrequited love. Jeremy will become a victim of his own passion, the kind of revenge wished on a lover by Eliza Acton, the cookbook writer and poet.

Revenge (1826)
by Eliza Acton

I would not, in the wildness of revenge,
Give poison to mine enemy, nor strike
My dagger to his heart, but I would plant
Love—burning—hopeless—and unquenchable—
Within the inmost foldings of his breast,
And bid him die the dark, and ling'ring death,
Of the pale victims, who expire beneath
The pow'r of that deep passion. Earth can show
No bitterness like this!—The shroud of thought
Which gathers round them, gloomy as the grave;—
The wasting, but unpitied pangs, which wear
The frame away, and make the tortur'd mind

Almost a chaos in its agony;—
The writings of the spirit, doom'd to see
A rival bless'd;—and utter, cold, despair:—
These are its torments!—Are they not enough
To satisfy the most remorseless hate?

Or Pomme could write a roman à clef, like Louise Colet's *Lui*,
an autobiographical novel with the abuses of her former lover,
Flaubert, filling its pages, publicly, embarrassingly. She might lock
Jeremy in a cellar like Poe's, with a cask of Amontillado, making
him feel indulged for a while and then desperate when he realizes
that he cannot escape. She could easily ignore his screams.

Voices clamor in Pomme's head. "Punishment is immoral
when the goal is revenge rather than correction," says Byron.
"What's the sense of learning how poisons work if one can't put the
knowledge to better use?" Baudelaire replies. "Something of vengeance I had tasted for the first time," says Jane Eyre. "An aromatic
wine it seemed, one swallowing, warm and racy, its first after-
flavour, metallic and corroding, gave me a sensation as if I had been
poisoned."

Pomme slams *Jane Eyre* shut. If revenge is a poison that tastes
like absinthe, Pomme knows that her reckless mood will destroy her
as well. Flaubert knew this too. In a letter to a friend, he wrote that
"the taste of arsenic was so real in my mouth when I described how
Emma Bovary was poisoned, that it cost me two indigestions one
upon the other—quite real ones, for I vomited my dinner." Pomme
fears the sickly sweet taste of revenge, delicious at first but now
lingering sour in her throat. She tears up the shopping list on which
she had written filé, mushrooms, almonds, and cream. She intends
to abandon this perverse obsession.

Jeremy had sounded an early warning, telling her that one day
he would break her heart. Pomme had laughed, thinking him

arrogant and bold. Later, why did she ignore the signs of his betrayal? She thinks about Hadley Hemingway who, in the winter of 1926, received a letter from Pauline, the woman who would soon destroy her marriage. "I've seen your husband E. Hemingway several times—sandwiched in like good red meat between thick slices of soggy bread. I think he looks swell, and he has been splendid to me." How could Hadley have ignored Pauline's intentions?

"When it comes to women, modern men are idiots," said D. H. Lawrence. "They don't know what they want, and so they never want, permanently, what they get. They want a cream cake that is at the same time ham and eggs and at the same time porridge. They are fools. If only women weren't so bound by fate to play up to them." In that case, Pomme says to herself, modern women are idiots too, and I have played along for too long, and I should never have yielded my heart and my mind so easily. "Passion will obscure our senses so that we eat sad stuff and call it nectar," wrote William Carlos Williams. I will reclaim my passion for myself, Pomme thinks.

In her solitude Colette learned to use precious time alone to reshape her perception. Pomme will no longer punish herself merely because she is alone and without a lover, nor dwell on the loss of love. She will not regret that the ripe curve of her mouth is wasted. She begins to prepare a comforting meal for one and to take pleasure in her own company. If austerity is the companion of solitude, then Pomme will choose foods that are simple and honest. She will not overindulge herself, lapsing into a depressed state of gluttony. The meal, pleasantly light, will nourish Pomme while she plans her future. She'll take her life-learned creativity and passion away from London, away from Jeremy and his unappreciative palate, away from Paris and its association with her loneliness, perhaps traveling as far away as America, searching to restore herself, to learn how to love without losing herself. "Oh, the pleasure of eating my dinner alone!" wrote the poet and essayist Charles Lamb to Mrs. Wordsworth. And with that, Pomme returns to her books and to her kitchen.

"On Being Alone," 1919
Journal of Katherine Mansfield

Saturday: This joy of being alone. What is it? I feel so gay and at peace—the whole house takes the air. Lunch is ready. I have a baked egg, apricots and cream, cheese straws and black coffee. How delicious! A baby meal! Athenaeum is asleep and then awake on the studio sofa. He has a silver spoon of cream—then hides under the sofa frill and puts out a paw for my finger. I gather the dried leaves from the plant in the big white bowl, and because I must play with something, I take an orange up to my room and throw it and catch it as I walk up and down. . . .

Why do cats frequent our visions of solitary comfort, Pomme wonders as she idly strokes Puss and eats from a cluster of hothouse grapes, the greenish amber ones that Léa ate as she mourned her lover's marriage to another woman in Colette's *Chéri*. She looks for a recipe for Mansfield's baked eggs and cheese straws.

BAKED EGG OR OEUF EN COCOTTE
Adapted from *Household Cookery,* Isabella Beeton, 1923 edition

Preheat oven to 350°F.

Butter a ramekin (or cocotte) and season with salt, cayenne, and chopped parsley. Break one egg into the ramekin.

Place the ramekin in a bain-marie (or pan of water) in the oven

and bake for 6 to 8 minutes. The yolk will be soft, the whites just set.
The ramekin will continue to cook the egg when it has been removed
from the oven, so be careful not to overcook.

Variations from *Larousse Gastronomique*

Pour 1 tablespoon of boiling cream into the ramekin. After breaking the egg on top of the cream, place a knob of butter on top. After
cooking, add salt and pepper or a sprinkling of Parmesan cheese. For
egg en cocotte à la tartare, mix ground raw beef with chopped chives,
salt, and pepper. Put a layer of the mixture into a buttered ramekin and
break the egg on top. Pour fresh cream around the yolk. Then bake
in a bain-marie.

CHEESE STRAWS
Adapted from *Household Cookery,* Isabella Beeton, 1923 edition

5 ounces flour
pinch of salt
pinch of cayenne pepper
½ cup butter
4 ounces grated Parmesan cheese
2 ounce grated cheddar or Cheshire cheese
2 egg yolks
1 tablespoon cold water

Preheat oven to 400°F.
Mix the flour and cheese. Rub in butter. Add salt and pepper to
taste.
Add egg yolks and enough cold water to form a stiff dough. Roll

dough into thin strips about 4 inches long and ⅛ inch wide. Bake on greased baking sheet for 10 minutes until crisp.

How poignantly Katherine Mansfield described her solitary meal, a baby meal, like a meal for a child, small and simple. How natural that comforting foods evoke images of an ideal childhood, of the best things about being a child, like buttered toast and honey, like Kenneth Grahame's *The Wind in the Willows:*

> The smell of buttered toast simply talked to Toad, and with no uncertain voice; talked of warm kitchens, of breakfasts on bright frosty mornings, of cosy parlour firesides on winter evenings, when one's ramble was over and slippered feet were propped on the fender; of the purring of contented cats, and the twitter of sleepy canaries.

Or like Henry Miller's recollection of being served a slice of home-made bread with butter and sugar smeared over it. "With a piece of bread like that I used to sit and read *Pinocchio* or *Alice Through the Looking Glass* or Hans Christian Andersen or *The Heart of a Boy,*" he wrote. Or like *The House at Pooh Corner:*

> And "What do you like best in the world, Pooh?"
> "Well," said Pooh, "what I like best . . ." and then he had to stop and think. Because although Eating Honey was a very good thing to do, there was a moment just before you began to eat it which was better than when you were, but he didn't know what it was called.

Pomme blends some honey with butter and a touch of cream to spread on warm toast, learning to care for herself even from

Pooh, who in his simple love for honey knows that the ache of anticipation is really the best moment of all. Is appetite like anticipation, once sated inevitably ending in disappointment, with surfeits of pleasure mounting toward certain indifference? When you're full, the last thing you want is more, Pomme knows. Jeremy had simply eaten his fill and left her alone with her simmering anger. Instead of greedily indulging her love, she should have teased the feeling along, allowing small feasts now and again but always preserving a keen balance between restraint and desire. Instead of the lavish pageant of exotic dishes, she should have fed him teas brewed from lady's mantle to excite his fading appetite, or doses of wormwood oil—two or three drops upon a sugar cube every few hours—to stimulate his waning heart. Just a little would have been enough. Too much would have been poison. If only she had known.

Tempting as they first sounded, Pomme is dissatisfied with buttered toast and honey, unsettled at the thought of retreating into childhood to find comfort. She is a grown woman and can comfort herself in a grown way. Much as she admires Katherine Mansfield, Pomme finds her solitary spirit a little too determined and forced, as though she's trying too hard to mask a deep unhappiness, a slow insidious toxin described in sad confidences in Mansfield's diary:

> . . . my anxious heart is eating up my body, eating up my nerves, eating up my brain. I feel this poison slowly filling my veins—every particle becoming slowly tainted . . .

> Late in the evening, after you have cleared away your supper, blown the crumbs out of the book that you were reading, lighted the lamp and curled up in front of the fire, that is the moment to beware of the rain.

No, what Pomme wants are true images of pleasure in solitude, the sight of Colette happily eating the biggest and the blackest cherries, taking the best for herself now that her lover has gone. She recalls the story of a woman named Lili whose lover, a cook, had abandoned her. Employed by Alice Toklas and Gertrude Stein, he had left behind one last piece of a special torte. Lili ate the cake and consoled herself with the balance of his wages, which Toklas and Stein promptly handed her. The cake cheered Lili, and so Pomme bakes herself a tender tart.

A TENDER TART

Adapted from *The Alice B. Toklas Cookbook,* Alice B. Toklas, 1954

Blend 5 ounces butter, 1 cup flour, and 1 egg yolk. Knead with enough water to hold dough together. Refrigerate for 30 minutes.

Beat 2 eggs and 1 cup sugar. Add 1 teaspoon vanilla and 1 cup ground hazelnuts and beat.

Roll out slightly more than half the dough, place in a greased pie dish, and fill with the hazelnut mixture. Roll out the remaining dough and cover the tart, crimping the edges together.

Bake for 30 minutes at 350°F.

Pomme sets a place for herself at the table while other, more pacific voices play in her mind. "In short, at the end of a good dinner, body and soul both enjoy a remarkable sense of well-being," the gastronomic philosopher Brillat-Savarin tells her, and suggests a soothing drink, a glass of warm milk with vanilla, the milk to induce gentle sleep and the vanilla to prompt light and agreeable dreams. Better still, a glass of new milk with a tablespoon of rum in it, along with thick mutton chops and two glasses a day of good sherry, the formula prescribed to Jane Carlyle by her doctor to prevent nervous collapse.

Pomme sautés a thick lamb chop, flavored with garlic—so good for the heart—and mint, a soothing herb. "After a good dinner one can forgive anybody, even one's own relations," says Oscar Wilde's Lady Caroline in *A Woman of No Importance*. Or even one's lovers, Pomme thinks, and bites into the meat, or even Jeremy. She nibbles on a slice of warm tender tart topped by a small scoop of icy Biscuits Tortoni.

Pomme reclines in a sleepy reverie, having dined simply but well and thinking of the future. Jeremy lingers at the fringe of her mind, a clear presence there still but more distant than before dinner. Colette whispers to Pomme about the time her first husband locked her in her room to force her to write, abandoning her for endless hours, day and night. "It taught me my most essential art," she tells Pomme, "which is not that of writing but the domestic task of knowing how to wait, to conceal, to save up crumbs, to reglue, regild, change the worst into the not-so-bad, how to lose and recover in the same moment that frivolous thing, a taste for life."

—·+··—

CHAPTER FIVE

Gastronomic Joylessness or Why Is the Food in England So Bad?

BY POMME BOUQUIN,
CULTURE AND CUISINE MAGAZINE

The English have one hundred religions, but only one sauce.

—Voltaire

'Damned fish glue', 'blasted frog spawn' 'Revolting! Like uncooked dough.'

—Joseph Conrad,
on porridge

One cannot think well, love well, sleep well if one has not dined well. The lamp in the spine does not light on beef and prunes.

—Virginia Woolf
A Room of One's Own

*W*hen I moved to New York from London last year and started work in the kitchens of one of the city's better hotels, I was surprised by my colleagues' hostility toward British cookery, a cuisine that has earned an enduring universal reputation for poverty in taste and spirit. Raised at the Savoy Hotel in London where my father is chef, my palate escaped the worst abuses of British cuisine. I had often wondered whether British cookery is really *that* bad and if so, why? How did Britain, a nation with excellent supplies of fresh fish, meats, fruits, and vegetables, develop a cuisine that leaves discriminating palates hungry for anything other than British food? I went back to visit England intending to find good food. I was in for a shock.

When I took the train into London, I recalled E. M. Forster's article in *Wine and Food* magazine about his own return to England. Arriving, perhaps, from some far-flung exotic place like India or Egypt, he took the London boat train and waited in the restaurant car, anxious for other passengers to board so that breakfast could be served. Waves of hunger destroyed his concentration for anything but food.

> At last the engine gave a jerk, the knives and forks slid sideways and sang against one another sadly, the cups said "cheap, cheap" to the sauces, as well they might, the door swung open and the attendants came in crying "Porridge or Prunes, Sir? Porridge or Prunes?" Breakfast had begun.
>
> That cry still rings in my memory. It is an epitome— not, indeed, of English food, but of the forces which drag it into the dirt. It voices the true spirit of gastronomic joylessness. Porridge fills the Englishman up, prunes clear him out, so their functions are opposed. But their spirit is the same: they eschew pleasure and consider delicacy immoral. That

morning they looked as like one another as they could. Everything was grey. The porridge was in pallid grey lumps, the prunes swam in grey juice like the wrinkled skulls of old men, grey mist pressed against the grey windows. "Tea or Coffee, Sir?" rang out next, and then I had a haddock. It was covered with a sort of hard yellow oilskin, as if it had been out in a lifeboat, and its insides gushed salt water when pricked. Sausages and bacon followed this disgusting fish. They, too, had been up all night. Toast like steel, marmalade a scented jelly. And the bill, which I paid dumbly, wondering again why such things have to be.

Forster published his breakfast lament in 1939, but worse quickly followed. Food rationing began in the following year and endured for fourteen more, loading the dining tables of England with powdered eggs, dried skim milk, ersatz butter, and tripe or sheep's belly. Mention tripe today and strike horror in the heart of anyone who lived in England during the war when platefuls of quivering boiled sheep's stomach in sauces of skim milk and onions were routinely dished up. Makeshift diets produced a generation of Britons overfamiliar with a mirthless cuisine, passively willing to accept less than the best in the food served them even in the years following the war.

War provides a reason for unpalatable food. Simone de Beauvoir wrote about wartime Paris and the appalling task of picking through food to remove maggots from parts still edible. Even so, M. F. K. Fisher's marvelous *How to Cook a Wolf,* inspired by wartime economy in the kitchen, exposes the flimsiness of the excuse with an array of recipes that transform meager ingredients into simple feasts. No, if we are to believe Forster, deep-seated qualities in the British character—a passive nature and Puritanical attitude toward pleasure—perpetuate the serving up of bad food.

William Somerset Maugham said that the only way to cope with England's cooking is to order breakfast three times a day. Clearly, Forster's porridge and prunes is not the meal that Maugham envisioned, but he might have imagined freshly grilled sausage and bacon, fried eggs, grilled mushrooms and tomatoes, a thick slice of wholemeal or Irish soda bread, or a bowl of steaming hot (properly cooked) porridge, followed by smoked haddock. The traditional, high-fat, high-protein breakfast, loaded with energy to combat the nation's notorious dampness, is where the idea that all British food tastes bad begins to break down.

I wonder about perpetrators of gastronomic joylessness, those people who choose to serve grey porridge and prunes rather than a traditional and delicious English breakfast. Are they merely ignorant, or should I blame their crimes on indifference? "Home to dinner, and there I took occasion, from the blackness of the meat as it came out of the pot, to fall out with my wife and my maid for their sluttery," wrote Samuel Pepys in his diary, immortalizing his wife for her failure in the kitchen. I hope that Elizabeth Pepys's actions were deliberate rather than the result of either indifference or ignorance, or that she was exacting a form of culinary revenge against her husband for his philandering ways. On November 13, 1660, not having learned the relative heat of her oven, Elizabeth, age twenty and married to Samuel for five years, overbaked her tarts and pyes, and again Samuel couldn't resist describing the spoiled food in his journal. Elizabeth may have fussed and planned and done what she could to prepare a fine meal, but she became the victim of what writer Zora Neale Hurston several centuries later called the kitchen-dwelling fiend, a demon who slips a scorched, soggy, tasteless mess into the pots and pans. In Hurston's novel *Their Eyes Were Watching God,* Janey's husband slaps her for spoiling the meal, another man who deserved his culinary punishment.

The Pepys family enjoyed eating despite the occasional crises in the kitchen and unreliable food supplies. Butter often tasted rancid in those days, and only a cacophony of spices—ginger, sugar, cloves, cinnamon, and saffron—could mask the taint of rotten meats. Pepys's diaries mention an array of foods and drinks virtually unknown today that S. A. E. Ström in *And So to Dine* identifies:

Botargo—a strongly salted form of caviar made from tunny or millet

Umbles baked in a pie—the liver, kidney, and heart of deer

Lambswool—a traditional Christmas drink made from hot ale, spiced and mixed with apple pulp

Sack posset—a milk curdled with ale and wine, usually sherry[1]

Wigges—caraway flavored biscuits

Foods more familiar to our taste today unnerved Pepys. In 1669, he worried that the pint of orange juice he had just consumed would harm him.

While Pepys faulted his wife's kitchen sluttery, he also praised her hashed pullets, ribs of beef, and pyes, so we can't imagine Elizabeth Pepys as emblematic of the bad cooks of England. No, the real criminals in the kitchen, like the cooks on Forster's boat train, are those who carelessly set down unappetizing, poorly cooked food before a hungry guest or customer, uninterested in learning how to do their job better. A popular cookbook of the 1700s called *The Art of Cookery,* by A Lady, warned the English that "most people spoil garden things by over boiling them." I wish more cooks in England had heeded her caution. Overboiled vegetables have become a hallmark of British food. With gruels, soups, and stews the staples of British diets for centuries, boiling has become generally associated with British cookery. In culinary parlance, boiling is a method described as à l'anglaise.

Like Forster, recall the worst meal of your life, an occasion when you were treated to the slack efforts of an indifferent cook. Mine was served in a Scottish restaurant, a Trout Rob Roy, a fish coated in oatmeal and fried to resemble cardboard in look, texture, and taste. When I sent the fish back to the kitchen, the waitress regarded me with dumb shock. I had the sad impression that everyone who ordered Trout Rob Roy ate it, glumly, with no thought of complaining. Does your own experience of a terrible meal compare to that? Or to the aggressively awful bread-and-butter served to George Orwell at a boardinghouse in Road to Wigan Pier?

> And like all people with permanently dirty hands he had a peculiarly intimate, lingering manner of handling things. If he gave you a slice of bread-and-butter there was always a black thumb print on it.

> For tea there was more bread-and-butter and frayed-looking sweet cakes which were probably bought as "stales" from the baker. For supper there was the pale flabby Lancashire cheese and biscuits. They always referred to them reverently as "cream crackers"—"Have another cream cracker, Mr. Reilly. You'll like a cream cracker with your cheese"—Thus glozing over the fact that there was only cheese for supper.

British public schools, mired in the same miserly culinary tradition as the boardinghouses, are notorious purveyors of bad food. Students over the centuries have waited impatiently for salvation in food hampers sent from home. Charles Lamb complained about the bad stew served at Christ's Hospital when he and Samuel Taylor Coleridge were pupils there in the late 1700s. Max Beerbohm recalled his eager anticipation of a care package filled with sausage rolls, while his friends awaited their own supplies of marmalade, sardines, and potted meat. (Potting is a method of preserving meat or fish by sealing the food with fat to prevent bacteria from entering.) The cooks at the underendowed women's college in Woolf's *A Room of One's Own* prepared a dismal meal of plain gravy soup and beef with greens and potatoes "suggesting the rumps of cattle in a muddy market, and sprouts curled and yellowed at the edge, and bargaining and cheapening." Prunes and custard followed, the prunes "stringy as a miser's heart."

Gastronomic indifference married to closefistedness spawns culinary horrors as well as the spurious belief that an abundance of food, no matter the quality, must therefore be good. Miserliness also destroys the very idea of cuisine. Food writer Jane Grigson once said that the image of Oliver Twist's workhouse gruel has spoiled the notion of soup in England forever. If indifference, ignorance, and miserliness are not the culprits spoiling a meal, then you can bet that their fussy cousin—pretentiousness—is on hand to meddle with the cooking pots.

In Anthony Trollope's novel *Miss Mackenzie* (1865), a woman hosts a fashionable dinner party à la Russe, a style that required a large staff of servants to deliver many elaborate dishes to the diners, who were allowed to do nothing for themselves. At Mrs. Mackenzie's dinner, a tyrannical headwaiter terrorizes the kitchen staff, creating needless delays that render the meal cold and greasy, typical in large drafty houses where servants brought food up from the lower kitchens. The excessive number of dishes included soup, fish, a saddle of mutton, a pair of boiled fowls, tongue, dessert, more:

> Why tell of the ruin, of the maccaroni, of the fine-colored pyramids of shaking sweet things which nobody would eat, and by the non-consumption of which nothing was gained, as they all went back to the pastrycook's,—or of the ice-pudding flavoured with onions? It was all misery, wretchedness, and degradation. Grandairs was king, and Mrs. Mackenzie was the lowest of his slaves. And why? . . . Her place in the world was fixed and she made no contest as to the fixing. She hoped for no great change in the direction of society. Why on earth did she perplex her mind and bruise her spirit, by giving a dinner à la anything? Why did she not have the roast mutton alone, so that all her guests might have eaten and been merry?

When Jane Welsh Carlyle, the wife of Thomas Carlyle, dined at the Dickens home she expressed similar scorn for their "fashionable" approach to food. In a letter to her cousin, Jane wrote: "Such getting up of the steam is unbecoming to a literary man who ought to have his basis elsewhere than on what the old Annandale woman called 'Ornament and grander.' The dinner was served up in the new fashion—not placed on the table at all—but handed round—only the dessert on the table and quantities of artificial flowers—but such an overloaded dessert! pyramids of figs raisins oranges—ach!"

Pretentiousness has blinded the British to good cookery and true hospitality. Pepys recorded the cost of meals that he served his friends throughout his diary. He also calculated what they spent on him at their own entertainments as a way to measure his social status. A century later, the stylish set hired French cooks freshly escaped from the fallen aristocratic homes of the French Revolution, no matter their qualifications. In *English Food,* Jane Grigson wrote that English food obtained publicly today is not bad British food but a "pretentious and inferior imitation of French and Italian cooking."

Food writer Elizabeth David acknowledged that while the English must be getting tired of hearing how cooking is an art and that the French have perfected it, the English should learn that the art of cooking is the discipline of leaving well enough alone. Taking as her example a simple Provençal meal of pâté, a gratin of courgettes and rice, a daube of beef sauced with a wine and tomato purée, and a dessert of jam, she describes how that same meal would be spoiled in an English kitchen by the addition of unnecessary flavors and presented with a concept of sophistication that would ruin the meal's innate simplicity.

Although a few brave souls have praised British cuisine, citing the high quality and variety of raw materials available in England, even they regretfully admit the difficulty of finding good food. Charles Cooper's *The English Table in History and Literature,* published at the turn of this century, staunchly defended English cookery, but Cooper, an honest man, is forced to concede in an endearing, wistful understatement that the English do not make the best use of vegetables. Writers like Cooper are lonely voices in the longstanding critical tradition of heaping scorn on British food. Other writers with enormous audiences—certainly larger than Cooper's—have busily propagated the nastiness of English food for centuries. Charles Dickens denounced the decline of West End chops and steaks. Nathaniel Hawthorne vociferously spoke out against the quality of life in English hotels, the joints and meat pies served there reminding him of other people's dinner scraps. Anthony Trollope, in 1862, found English inns similarly lacking in welcome, serving tough beef and inferior port.

But these writers, as well as Forster, condemned food served in public places in Britain, which bears little resemblance to home-cooked meals or to the hearty foods of the countryside. Country recipes, rather than cheap imitations of what the British imagine to be elegant Continental cuisine, are the heart of the quiet tradition of good food in England. Practitioners of a falsely elaborate style of cooking would eradicate the British reputation for poor food if they aspired instead to simplicity, a return to honest and good cookery, perhaps taking a lesson from Celia Fiennes (1662–1741). In her travel diary, published in 1888 as *Through England on a Side Saddle in the Time of William and Mary,* Fiennes marveled at how food in the countryside is more delicious (fresher) and less expensive (no transport costs) than meals found in London. She raves about Fruite Sweetemeetes, Gingerbread sold at markets, golden trout, and potted fish.[2] Celia also had a sweet tooth:

> When in the town of St. Austins . . . my landlady brought me one of the West Country tarts . . . its an apple pye with a custard all on the top, its the most acceptable entertainment that could be made me; they scald their creame and milk in most parts of those countrys and so its a sort of clouted creame as we call it, with a little sugar, and soe put on the top of the apple pye . . .[3]

Syllabub, a dessert made from wine blended with cream, was another popular country dish occasionally still served today. A version of the recipe in *The Cook and Housewife's Manual,* by Meg Dods, published in 1819, with footnotes credited to Sir Walter Scott, calls for the cook to milk a cow directly into the bowl of liquor:

> Sweeten a pint of port, and another of Madeira or sherry, in a china bowl. Milk about three pints of milk over this. In a

short time it will bear clouted cream laid over it. Grate nutmeg over this, and strew a few coloured comfits on top if you choose.

In 1808 Jane Austen, who prepared the family's breakfasts and managed the household's stores of tea, sugar, and wine, wrote to Althea Biggs in London asking for the recipe for a version of syllabub made with Seville oranges.[4]

A country dish that has largely disappeared is furmity or frumenty, a fermented and sweetened grain eaten in place of porridge. Laced with rum, furmity put Michael Henchard in a drunken temper, and he auctioned his wife and child in Thomas Hardy's *The Mayor of Casterbridge* (1886). Hardy describes the potent dish:

> For furmity . . . was nourishing, and as proper a food as could be obtained within the four seas; though, to those not accustomed to it, the grains of wheat swollen as large as lemon-pips, which floated on its surface, might have a deterrent effect at first.

Furmity is made by soaking whole-wheat or barley grains in water for several days, keeping the bowl in a warm place. When the grains swell and burst, releasing starch, the mixture becomes a thick jelly in which the grains are suspended. The furmity is then stirred hot with honey or sugar and warm milk, or with raisins and currants.[5] Like furmity, many British country dishes took advantage of the fermenting and rotting properties of meats, grains, and milk to make delicious dishes that seem strange to us today with our advanced methods of cold storage and preservation.

Hawthorne may have lamented the joints and meat pies served in restaurants, but many fine recipes exist for English Sunday family dinners—lunch to Americans—including Yorkshire pudding, roast potatoes, and mashed parsnips. Other classic Sunday lunches might include boiled beef with carrots, pease pudding (puréed peas with butter), dumplings, roast beef, mutton served with mint sauce or jelly, or roast pork with crackling and applesauce, with many regional variations, foods that I would invite poor Forster to share to remove the taste of prunes from his mouth.[6] And while Oliver Twist may have spoiled the notion of soup in England, Dickens also created culinary legends of traditional dishes such as roasted goose and Christmas pudding. In *A Christmas Carol,* the figs are moist and pulpy, French plums blush, modestly hiding their tartness under a sugary coat, and candied fruits—caked and spotted with molten sugar—make even the coldest lookers-on feel faint. The Cratchit family waits breathlessly for the carving knife to plunge into the breast of the roasted goose and sighs when the stuffing bursts forth, and when the Cratchits are filled to the eyebrows with sage and onion, the Christmas pudding is brought in "like a speckled cannon-ball, so hard and firm, blazing in half of half-a-quartern of ignited brandy, and bedight with Christmas holly stuck in the top."

Then there is also the lascivious pleasure of the traditional English cream tea. The high tea, thought to be started in England by the Duchess of Bedford in the 1830s as a snack between an early lunch and a late supper, earned the scorn of the Radical Parliamentarian and writer William Cobbett, who pronounced that "the gossip of the tea table is no bad preparatory school for the brothel." Yet Cobbett's own popular book, *Cottage Economy,* published in the early 1800s and kept in print for many decades, offered recipes that would have been perfect for teatime, including one for a lemon and orange-flower cake.[7] *Cottage Economy* emphasizes the pleasures of simple and rustic foods, of home-baked breads, of country cooking. (Cobbett's appreciation for countryfolk went only so far. He described watching "a great heavy fellow in a bakehouse in France, kneading bread with his *naked feet!* His feet looked very white to be sure: whether they were of that color *before he got into the trough* I could not tell. God forbid that I should suspect that this is ever done *in England!"*)

I have prepared traditional English dishes at home and smiled at the pleasure on my guest's face as he dabbed the last of the gravy from the corners of his mouth. But when I have wanted to dine out in England, I've had to launch an expedition to locate a decent restaurant. "We do not demand good food in public," said Forster, "and when we eat upon an object that moves, such as a train or a boat, we expect, and generally get, absolute muck." Forster doubted that the good food of England could appear more frequently or more reliably on the nation's public dining tables. Complaining won't help, he said, because the system doesn't understand how you feel.

You'll understand why Forster felt that the British are married to the systems they've created when you arrive at a pub on a blistering cold day a scant two minutes after the end of lunch hour and are refused even a simple ploughman's lunch—a cold plate of bread, cheese, and pickled onions. "Sorry, love, the kitchen's closed," is what you'll be told. But Ford Madox Ford, who for a time supervised the cooks of His Britannic Majesty's Expeditionary Force, claimed that if he is able to find acceptable food, then anyone can. "That is because if I may express a he-man's sentiments in soldierly language I damn well see that I get it," he said. The British, not knowing that they are entitled to demand good food in Ford's good soldierly fashion, have tacitly sanctioned the appearance of unpleasant meals on their restaurant tables.

Even the quality of food served in British homes is uneven, sometimes tainted by a stubborn Puritan streak that permeates the culture. Jessie Conrad's cookbooks, *A Handbook of Cookery for a Small House* and *Home Cookery,* open with an introduction by her husband, Joseph, discussing the virtues of good cooking as a moral agent. "By good cooking I mean the conscientious preparation of the simple food of every-day life," he wrote, "not the more or less skillful concoction of idle feasts and rare dishes. Conscientious cooking is an enemy to gluttony." The search for simplicity in food can be taken too far, and a utilitarian tone dominates the cookbooks. Jessie's preface establishes a series of strict and discouraging rules for the home cook:

> Cooking ought not to take too much of one's time. One hour and a half to two hours for lunch, and two and a half for dinner is sufficient. . . . But once the cooking is begun one must give all one's attention and care to it. No dish, however simple, will cook itself. You must not leave the kitchen while the cooking is going on—unless of necessity and only for a very few minutes at a time.
>
> The bane of life in a small house is the smell of cooking. Very few are free from it. And yet it need not be endured at all. This evil yields to nothing more heroic than a simple but scrupulous care in all the processes in making food ready for consumption. That is why your constant presence in the kitchen is recommended.

A distinct lack of sensuousness emerges in Jessie's books as she reveals how to get rid of bad smells and leftovers, two points with which she is consumed. Don't put a pan that has been used to cook eggs and bacon into the sink as the cold water will cause it to smell unpleasantly, she advises. Kippers are more problematic, but the enterprising Jessie recommends a combined frying and baking method that eliminates all odors.

John Conrad's memoir of his father explains that Joseph became difficult when he didn't like his meal, demanding

that it be "properly cooked next time" when it was sent back
to the kitchen. . . . He loathed porridge for which he had
a variety of names: "damned fish glue", "blasted frog
spawn" "Revolting! Like uncooked dough". His antipathy
to it was largely due to the uninviting colour and consistency
of the usual hotel variety of those days. . . . Though my
mother made bread sauce in a special way which was acceptable, JC never really liked it any more than he liked a boiled
chicken, which he considered to be a waste of good food.

JESSIE CONRAD'S RECIPE FOR
BREAD SAUCE

Peel and cut into quarters one onion and let it simmer in a pint of milk
till perfectly tender. Break one fourth pound stale bread into small
pieces or grate it into crumbs, put it into a clean saucepan and strain
the milk from the onion over it; cover it with the lid and let it remain
an hour to soak. Beat it briskly with a fork, add a little salt, a small
pinch of cayenne pepper, and either a little cream or a piece of butter
the size of a walnut.

Joseph, with his picky appetite and reproachful temper, and
Jessie, with her pragmatic approach to cooking, emphatically banish
from their home the idea that cooking and eating are pleasurable
activities. I wish the Conrad household was a unique culinary
curiosity. Earlier, in 1851, a small cookbook appeared called *What
Shall We Have for Dinner,* by Lady Maria Clutterbuck, a playful
pseudonym for Catherine Hogarth, the wife of Charles Dickens.
Dickens, who described more elaborate foods in his books than
most novelists consume in their lifetime, must have loathed the
stodgy, pedestrian fare found in his wife's book.

Like Forster, Gregory Bowden in *British Gastronomy* suggests that it is primarily the Puritan heritage that has spoiled the food in England, making talking and thinking about food seem sinful, banning sumptuous traditional Christmas foods as abominations, and forbidding the use of spices because they excite passion. Ample literary and culinary evidence backs Bowden's claim. Samuel Johnson, known for his greed, berated himself for his weakness in his journal. "I have made no reformation; I have lived totally useless, more sensual in thought, and more addicted to wine and meat," he wrote. He gave up wine during the last twelve years of his life, but substituted chocolate stirred with great quantities of butter and cream. As a child, Walter Scott once enjoyed a meal excessively, an act considered wickedly sensual by his father, who poured cold water into the soup to drown the devil. "An Englishman thinks he is moral when he is only uncomfortable," George Bernard Shaw wrote in *Man and Superman.* Does the pleasure-denying component of the Puritan legacy make us proclaim ourselves sinners today when we indulge in a particularly caloric and high-fat dessert? Or prompt some among us to cluck happily with disapproval at the self-indulgence of others?

If we are what we eat, did the individuals in history and literature with a reputation for sourness and spite—like Oliver Cromwell, like Scrooge—turn out the way they did because they didn't enjoy their food? Were they raised on bad food, never to purge its poisonous effect from their souls and minds? Have a disproportionate number of curdled souls dominated British cooking?

If only the British would stop serving prunes and stick to what they do well—scones and crumpets with steaming pots of tea, roast meats and Yorkshire puddings at Sunday lunch, game pies and potted foods and other hearty meals served at rustic inns that seem unnecessarily hard to locate. There is good food in England, you just have to be willing to work hard to find it. Clearly, E. M. Forster was on the wrong train.

———⊷⊰≈❀≈⊱⊶———

1 . SACK POSSET

In *Consuming Passions,* Phillipa Pullar provides a recipe for sack posset left by Sir Walter Raleigh. His recipe called for boiling ½ pint each of sherry and ale and gradually adding 1 quart of boiling cream or milk. The mixture was then sweetened, flavored with nutmeg, and left to stand by a fire for several hours.

Claret or orange juice were sometimes used to make posset. According to C. Anne Wilson in *Food and Drink in Britain,* the addition of breadcrumbs to an ale or beer posset produced an eating posset. A richer version called for the addition of eggs, grated biscuits, or almonds.

2 . TO POT SALMON
From *The Art of Cookery Made Plain and Easy,* Hannah Glasse, 1774

Take a piece of fresh salmon, scale it, and wipe it clean, (let your piece or pieces be as big as will lie cleverly on your pot) season it with Jamaica pepper, black pepper, mace, and cloves beat fine, mixed with salt, a little sal prunella, beat fine, and rub the bone with. Season with a little of the spice, pour clarified butter over it, and bake it well. Then take it out carefully, and lay it to drain; when cold, season it well, lay it in your pot close, and cover it with clarified butter.

Thus you may do carp, tench, trout, and several sorts of fish.

3 . TO MAKE AN APPLE PIE
From *The Art of Cookery Made Plain and Easy,* Hannah Glasse, 1774

Make a good puff paste crust, lay some round the sides of the dish, pare and quarter your apples, and take out the cores, lay a row of apples thick, throw in half the sugar you design for your pie, mince a little lemon-peel fine, throw over and squeeze a little lemon over them, then a few cloves, here and there one, then the rest of your apples and the rest of your sugar. You must sweeten to your palate, and squeeze a little more lemon. Boil the peeling of the apples and cores in some fair water, with a blade of mace, till it is very good; strain it and boil the syrup with a little sugar, till there is but very little and good, pour it into your pie, put on your upper crust and bake it. You may put in a little quince or marmalade if you please.

Thus make a pear pie, but don't put in any quince. You may butter them when they come out of the oven: or beat up the yolks of two eggs and half a pint of cream, with a little nutmeg, sweetened with sugar, take off the lid and pour in the cream. Cut the crust in little three-corner pieces, stick about the pie and send it to table.

PUFF-PASTE
From *The Art of Cookery Made Plain and Easy,* Hannah Glasse, 1774

Take a quarter of a peck of flour, rub fine half a pound of butter, a little salt, make it up into a light paste with cold water, just stiff enough to work it well up; then roll it out, and stick pieces of butter all over, and strew a little flour; roll it up and roll it out again; and so do nine or ten times, till you have rolled in a pound and a half of butter. This crust is mostly used for all sorts of pies.

CUSTARD SAUCE FOR SWEET PUDDINGS OR TARTS
Adapted from *Beeton's Book of Household Management,* Isabella Beeton, 1859–1861

1 pint of milk
2 eggs
3 oz. of sugar
1 tablespoon of brandy
nutmeg

Put the milk in a saucepan, and bring to a boil. Beat the eggs, stir in the milk and add sugar, and put the mixture into a jug. Place the jug in a saucepan of boiling water; keep stirring well until it thickens, but do not allow it to boil, or it will curdle. Serve the sauce in a tureen, stir in the brandy, and grate a little nutmeg over the top.

CLOUTED CREAM (OR CLOTTED CREAM)
From *The Art of Cookery Made Plain and Easy,* Hannah Glasse, 1774

Take a gill of new milk, and set it on the fire, and take six spoonfuls of rose-water, four or five pieces of large mace, put the mace on a thread; when it boils, put to them the yolks of two eggs very well beaten; stir them very well together; then take a quart of very good cream, put it to the rest, and stir it together, but let it not boil after the cream is in. Pour it out of the pan you boil it in, and let it stand all night; the next day take the top off it, and serve it up.

When the cream stands overnight, it forms a thick crust, which is then skimmed off. Eliza Acton—her cookbook *Modern Cookery for Private Families* was published one hundred years after Glasse's—explained that clotted cream may be converted to butter by beating it in a shallow wooden tub.

4. TO MAKE WHIPT SYLLABUBS
From *The Art of Cookery Made Plain and Easy,* Hannah Glasse, 1774

Take a quart of thick cream, and half a pint of sack, the juice of two Seville oranges or lemons, grate in the peel of two lemons, half a pound of double refined sugar, pour it into a broad earthen pan, and whisk it well; but first sweeten some red wine or sack, and fill your glasses as full as you chuse, then as the froth rises take it off with a spoon, and lay it carefully into your glasses till they are as full as they will hold. Don't make these long before you use them. Many use cyder sweetened, or any wine you please, or lemon, or orange whey made thus: squeeze the juice of a lemon or orange into a quarter of a pint of milk; when the curd is hard, pour the whey clear off, and sweeten it to your palate. You may colour some with the juice of spinach, some with saffron, and some with cochineal, just as your fancy.

5. TO MAKE FIRMITY
From *The Art of Cookery Made Plain and Easy,* Hannah Glasse, 1774

Take a quart of ready-boiled wheat, two quarts of milk, a quarter of a pound of currants clean picked and washed: stir these together and boil them, beat up the yolks of three or four eggs, a little nutmeg, with two or three spoonfuls of milk, add to the wheat; stir them together for a few minutes. Then sweeten to your palate, and send it to the table.

6. EXCELLENT HORSERADISH SAUCE (TO SERVE HOT OR COLD WITH ROAST BEEF)
From *Modern Cookery,* Eliza Acton, 10th edition, 1850

Wash and wipe a stick of young horseradish, grate it as small as possible on a fine grater, then with two ounces (or a couple of large tablespoonsful) of it, mix a small teaspoonful of salt, and four tablespoonsful of good cream; stir in briskly and by degree, three dessertspoonsful of vinegar, one of which should be Chili vinegar when the horseradish is mild. To heat the sauce, put it into a small and delicately clean saucepan, hold it over, but do not place it upon the fire, and stir it without intermission until it is near the point of simmering, but do not allow it to boil, or it will curdle instantly.

Horseradish pulp, 2 ozs. (or, 2 large tablespoonsful); salt, 1 teaspoonful; good cream, 4 tablespoonsful; vinegar, 3 dessertspoonsful (of which one should be Chili when the root is mild).

GOOD YORKSHIRE PUDDING
From *Modern Cookery,* Eliza Acton, 10th edition, 1850

To make a good and light Yorkshire pudding, take an equal number of eggs and of heaped tablespoonsful of flour, with a teaspoonful of salt to six of these. Whisk the eggs well, strain, and mix them gradually with the flour, then pour in by degrees as much new milk as will reduce the batter to the consistency of rather thin cream. The tin which is to receive the pudding must have been placed for some time previously under a joint that has been put down to roast: one of beef is usually preferred. Beat the batter briskly and lightly the instant before it is poured into the pan, watch it carefully that it may not burn, and let the edges have an equal share of the fire. When the pudding is quite firm in every part, and well-coloured on the surface, turn it to brown the under side. This is best accomplished by first dividing it into quarters. In Yorkshire it is made much thinner than in the south, roasted generally at an enormous fire, and not turned at all: currants there are sometimes added to it.

Eggs, 6; flour, 6 heaped tablespoonsful, or from 7 to 8 ozs.; milk, nearly or quite, 1 pint; salt, 1 teaspoonful: 2 hours.

7. RECIPES FOR
AN ENGLISH CREAM TEA

Foods served at teatime might include sandwiches, scones, or other cakes
and buns spread with jam and clotted cream.

A NICE CAKE
Adapted from *Cottage Economy,* William Cobbett, 1867

Break 3 eggs into a pan, put to them 6 ounces of cornmeal, 4 ounces of sugar,
the grated peel of a lemon, the yolks of five and the whites of 3 eggs, and a
tablespoonful of orange-flower water, beat it well for 20 minutes, pour it into
moulds, and bake the cakes three-quarters of an hour, of a light brown colour.

CRUMPETS
Adapted from *Beeton's Book of Household Management,* Isabella Beeton,
1859–1861

To every quart of milk allow 1½ ounces of German yeast, a little salt, flour.
   Warm the milk, add to it the yeast, and mix these well together; put them
into a pan and stir in sufficient flour to make the whole into a batter; cover it
over with a cloth and place it in a warm place to rise for about half an hour.
Pour it into iron rings, which should be ready on a hot plate; bake them, and
when one side appears done, turn them quickly on the other.
   To toast them, have ready a very bright clear fire; put the crumpet on a
tasting-fork, and hold it before the fire, not too close, until it is nicely brown
on one side. Turn it and brown the other side; then spread it with good butter.

VICTORIA SANDWICHES
From *Beeton's Book of Household Management,* Isabella Beeton, 1859–1861

4 eggs; their weight in pounded sugar, butter, and flour; ¼ saltspoonful
of salt, a layer of any kind of jam or marmalade.
   Beat the butter to a cream; dredge in the flour and pounded sugar; stir
these ingredients well together, and add the eggs, which should be previously
thoroughly whisked. When the mixture has been well beaten for about 10

minutes, butter a Yorkshire pudding tin, pour in the batter, and bake it in a moderate oven for 20 minutes. Let it cool, spread one half of the cake with a layer of nice preserve, place over it the other half of the cake, press the pieces slightly together, and then cut into long finger-pieces; pile them in cross-bars on a glass dish and serve.

~·+·✣✧✣✧✣·+·~

CHAPTER SIX

Starving Artists

THE PRISON DIARY OF POMME'S AMERICAN LOVER

*P*omme said the name Jeremy aloud in her sleep and awoke the next morning to propose that I take a trip alone. She had dreamed that solitude would help me, she told me, and that I should spend significant time alone to force myself to write my novel. I asked her who Jeremy was, and she looked startled and said only that he was a powerful man who taught her harsh and important lessons about art and love.

Now I am learning a lesson of my own. My solitude is no longer a choice, and I face possible starvation and life sentence in a Singaporean jail. My sole, occasional companion is an uncharming Malay jailer, who finally returned my notebooks and pens. "Arrested for drug smuggling?" I can hear the dean saying, suppressed glee in his voice at the unexpected gift, the perfect reason to deny my tenure. He deplores my passionate approach to teaching English literature to his precious undergraduates. Perhaps he had the marijuana planted in my bag.

Alexandre Dumas traveled in czarist Russia, thrilled that his novels and the works of his colleagues—Lamartine, Hugo, Balzac, Musset, Sand—were well known even there. My own travels have ended in lonely disaster. Others in the world must be unhappier and more hungry than I. Just now I can't think who they might be. I've been rotting here for weeks. The fall semester began yesterday.

Perhaps the university is simply ignoring the wire I sent. Perhaps they are doing everything they can to get me out, but I'd never know. When I demand information, the guard looks with uncomprehending eyes at the apparition in his custody.

Pomme told me that if I live vicariously through the lives of poets and adventurers, writers and wanderers, then I should have something to show for my obsession. For some reason, my creative light won't kindle, while hers blazes strong and bright. We've traveled together to gaze at the wonders of the world, inspired not by the beauty of the views, but by the idea that Flaubert stood here in the shadow of the Sphinx, or that Hemingway drank at this tavern when he was in town for the bull run, or that Byron climbed this Swiss mountain peak and stopped to eat thick slabs of shepherd's pie, a homely dish of ground beef and onion topped with a layer of mashed potatoes that Pomme has sometimes made for my dinner. I wanted to see this part of the world through the eyes of Auden and Isherwood, who took tea with the mysterious Madame Chiang Kai-shek. Madame touched nothing herself and inquired whether poets ate cake or preferred spiritual food. Poets' food is love and fame, Shelley once wrote, but Auden ate the cake. I saw myself like Conrad, Maugham, Forster, lounging on the porch of the Oriental Hotel, gently reclining with a cup of tea between adventures.

Until I met Pomme, my wanderings through the lives of writers seemed not a bad way to live. Like them I traveled East, carrying the same apricot paste that Alexandre Dumas described, dried in the sun and rolled up like a carpet and when boiled in water, an excellent marmalade. I too enjoyed Dumas's breakfast of camel's milk and rose jam made with honey and cinnamon, brought to me in my desert tent. I headed the "Harvard in Europe Program" one summer, following routes forged by Herman Melville and Nathaniel

Hawthorne, who themselves sought the pathways of our literary forebears. They slept at the Yacht Inn in Chester where Swift had stayed and at the Crown Inn in Oxford where Shakespeare used to stop on his way to Stratford. They traveled finally to Constantinople, Byron's final destination before he died from fever in 1814. And like John Dos Passos, I once walked with a woman through the Pyrenees, carrying goat cheese, black bread, honey, and tortilla to eat along the way, searching for the inn near Buguete to dine on thick garlic soup with eggs broken into it.

Until now I've held a romantic image of writers who starved in their Paris garrets. I admired their perseverance despite the constancy of hunger raging in their guts. Their deprivation must have indelibly marked their literature and their lives, formed them, shaped their outlook and taste, tested their dedication to their work. I thought them glamorous prisoners, serving a sentence until they proved their worth and then, if they were talented and lucky, breaking free to enjoy the full fruits of admiration and literary fame. Perhaps like those starving artists, my fate is to hunger until I have found my focus and then to be set loose with a renewed sense of purpose and commitment to finish my book. I would like to tell Pomme about this. She would be pleased for me.

The Malay has just shoved a plateful of dry curried rice under my door. Charles Baudelaire once said that in the absence of restaurants, the only consolation was reading cookbooks. In the absence of any food save a few grains of rice, I'll dream about the foods I might choose from an imaginary cookbook, like the one that Goethe described in his memoirs of the 1792 campaign in France. I am like his desperately hungry soldiers who greedily broke open a kitchen cabinet but found only a very fat cookbook. Their discovery mocked their hunger, but they sat around a fire and took turns reading aloud the most delicious recipes, pretending they were dining on fine food, "intensifying hunger and desire to the point of despair but exciting the imagination." I'll choose other writers to join me in a feast here in my cell, a modern-day Symposia. We'll sit back to drink and dine, we'll talk about women and love.

I am not the first person to starve to death, merely the latest. I used to laugh at Edmond de Goncourt's description of the Siege of Paris when the Prussians cut off all lines of supply into the city and food became gradually more scarce. In December of 1870, he wrote about visiting Roos', an English butcher's shop in Paris, where he was amused to find the skinned trunk of the zoo's baby elephant hanging from the wall, the animal's meat having been sold for food. For his lunch, Edmond passed over the camel's kidneys in favor of a couple of larks. A week later, he complained about the exorbitant prices for food, how half a pound of horse meat served as rations for two people for three days. "As for the two staple items of the diet of the poorer classes—potatoes and cheese," he wrote, "cheese is just a memory, and you have to have friends in high places to obtain potatoes at twenty francs a bushel." I no longer find Edmond's frustration very funny.

I teach the lives of writers to my students, hoping that if I bring them to life as personalities then their literature will resonate more significantly. I am happy when I spark the light in those young impatient eyes. Émile Zola, unknown in Paris in 1860 when he was the same age as my students, nearly starved. He lived on bread and watery soup and moved through his days in a stupor, the same kind of hunger-induced inertia that George Orwell later described in *Down and Out in Paris and London*. On a good day, Zola was able to buy a tiny piece of pork from the change he earned delivering visiting cards, or to trap a sparrow on his windowsill, and yet he continued to write poetry, sending an occasional letter to his friend Paul Cézanne. "I have few illusions, Paul," he wrote. "I know I can only stammer. But I'll find a way."

Zola was living in a filthy lodging hotel in Rue Soufflot, a louse-infested place inhabited by thieves and prostitutes. He felt ill and cold and hungry. "I feel a heaviness in my belly and in my bowels," he wrote. "My insides worry me, and so does the future." He wandered Les Halles, the food market that was bursting with smells of cheeses and fruits and meat and sweat, an experience that must have forced tears of frustration from Zola but later became a motif for his novel *The Belly of Paris.* Paul Cézanne's longed-for arrival proved a false promise of companionship in mutual artistic struggle. The painter became disillusioned about Paris's ability to inspire and soon returned to the South, leaving Zola to carry on alone. By 1862, Zola managed to publish some poetry and found a job in the shipping department of the Hachette publishing company.

More than thirty-five years later, after cultivating a gluttonous appetite and a marvelous girth, Zola wrote *J'Accuse,* protesting the verdict in the Dreyfus case, and was forced into exile in England where he complained about the bad food. He loathed England's insufficient salt and sauces, the watery vegetables, spongy bread, and bad desserts, and once had the unpleasant experience of biting unexpectedly on a clove baked into a cake. He had forgotten the lean days when he would have been grateful for any scrap. Were Zola to visit me for dinner, I would have him go to the Rue Saint-Lazare where it meets the Passage Tivoli to bring me the feast served in his honor at the Restaurant Trap on the night of April 13, 1877, the literary dinner regarded by some as the formal foundation of the Naturalist movement. Before I'll allow Zola to take even one bite, I'll make him sit quietly for a few moments to remember the time when he had nothing.

That April evening, the literary disciples of Zola—six men in their early twenties and some not even that old—gathered to salute "the three masters of modern literature," Flaubert, Zola, and Edmond de Goncourt, as Goncourt himself described it, although *his* fiction is largely forgotten. The menu served to this self-conscious group of men, who were committed to what they perceived as an important new, realistic style of literature, comprised Potage purée Bovary, truite saumonée à la fille Elisa, poularde truffée à la Saint-Antoine, artichauts au coeur simple, parfait naturaliste, vin de Coupeau, and liqueurs de L'Assommoir. "This is a new literary army taking shape," Goncourt wrote of the evening's tribute to Flaubert's *Madame Bovary, La Tentation de Saint Antoine,* and *Un Coeur Simple,* Zola's *L'Assommoir,* and his own *La Fille Elisa.*

Goncourt is not welcome in my cell. Jealous of Zola's success, he has made himself disagreeable to me in other ways. He once wrote: "What makes me think that people who practically starve to death or who have no security to look forward to, do not suffer as much as they are said to suffer, is that there is no bitterness in their works. It is in the works of rich men that you have to look for bitterness, in Byron, Musset, and Chateaubriand." I tell you, Monsieur Goncourt, a great deal of bitterness grows alongside hunger in the heart, mind, soul, and stomach of a person who starves.

Zola said that a "chaste writer can be immediately recognized by the fierce virility of his touch. He is filled with desires as he writes, and these desires prompt the outbursts in his great masterpieces." My physical deprivation should therefore provoke a muscular achievement in my work. Will starvation fuel my progress toward accomplishment and recognition?

Someone told Marcel Proust that the mind functions better on an empty stomach, compelling the author to starve himself for the sake of his work. "There was something sublime in this sacrifice of a mortal body to an immortal work," wrote André Maurois in *The World of Marcel Proust,* "in this transfusion where the donor chose deliberately to shorten his days for the sake of the characters who were taking his life's blood." Proust seemed to exist entirely on milk and the memory of childhood foods. He'd often describe in exquisite detail meals he had once enjoyed, but refused his housekeeper's offers to procure them. He avoided the disappointment that repeating an idealized experience often brings. "The only place where you can regain lost paradises . . . is in yourself," he told her.

Ceremonial and precise rituals accompanied Proust's abstemious diet—his morning café au lait and croissant placed carefully at his bedside (until 1914, when he stopped eating croissants altogether), a small meal of roast chicken and apple jelly served in bed with his friends gathered around when he was too ill to venture outside, an impromptu midnight meal of fried potatoes, or sole with thin slices of lemon presented on a clean linen napkin. When Proust dined out, he'd order fillets of sole in white wine, boeuf à la mode (despite the fact that this was one of the treasured meals of his past, a specialty of his parents' cook), and creamy chocolate soufflé. He ate little of them.

Like Proust, I knew myself to be among the elite—a popular professor due for tenure, adored by my students, maverick, slightly controversial, admired by a beautiful, strong woman who prepares exotic foods for me and tells me stories about food and love while I tell her stories about the lives of writers. Here, lonely and hungry in my cell, I am as poor, bereft, and insignificant as anyone else. I wish I had written my novel. I won't have Proust join me in my feast for starving artists. He depresses me.

But I would dearly like to meet Stephen Crane, who moved to England from the States and became a literary star for a brief bright time until he died from tuberculosis at the age of twenty-nine. His generosity and wide-eyed pleasure about his success make him charming, beguiling, despite the fact that the literary parasites considered him an easy mark. "Literary London of that day—I do not know how it may be now—was filled to about capacity by the most discreditable bums that any city can ever have seen," said Ford Madox Ford in *Portraits from Life*. After a short hard period when Crane first arrived in England—everything passed so quickly in this man's life—he began to earn the extravagant sum of twenty pounds for every thousand words he wrote. He bought hampers of foie gras and caviar and champagne and went to see Ford. They sat up all night celebrating Crane's good fortune. Ford later wrote:

> He was the son of an Episcopalian bishop and had been born indifferently in the Bowery or in Wyoming or on Pike's Peak. There were thus no flies on him, whereas I was simply crawling with them. . . . And he produced from the hip pocket of his riding-breeches into which he had changed from his town clothes, a Colt revolver, with the foresight of which he proceeded to kill flies. . . . He had spilt a little champagne over a lump of sugar on the table and flies had come in companies. He really did succeed in killing one, flicking the gun backhanded with his remarkably strong wrists.

Crane will make good company. Together we'll drink champagne and eat oysters while we shoot flies with our revolvers and not give a damn what anyone thinks. Crane understood the value of living his time well.

I will sleep now and dream of the restorative veau à la casserole served at least three times a week at the Café de Paris, praised by Balzac, and Dumas. The dish helped them recruit their mental and bodily strength.

• • •

What might I expect from my hunger? Has hunger blessed the world's starving artists with a sense of urgency about their work, or has it forced them to compromise their art in order to feed themselves? Has starvation sharpened their perceptions, widening their understanding of desire? "Science can analyse a pork chop, and say how much of it is phosphorus and how much is protein," said G. K. Chesterton, "but science cannot analyse any man's wish for a pork chop, and say how much of it is hunger, how much nervous fancy, how much a haunting love of the beautiful."

Hemingway, in his memoirs of living in Paris as a young man, described how hunger sharpens the senses, and is good for a writer, but Hemingway seemed to have experienced only a mild kind of hunger. Even in lean days he managed to get by, quelling his appetite with alcohol or with simple café meals like beer and new potatoes tossed in olive oil, perhaps with a few chopped shallots and parsley.

Hemingway had hunger enough to write but not so much that he couldn't enjoy Paris or reject writing assignments he thought beneath him. I suspect he did not experience the pangs of the deepest kind of hunger, at least not for food. He lived the kind of life in 1920s Paris that the journalist and gourmand A. J. Liebling also enjoyed, having just enough money to develop a discriminating palate without taking food for granted. Even when Liebling waited for his monthly stipend, he satisfied his inquiring appetite with andouilles (sausages made from pork), boudin (black sausage), biftek (steak), pot-au-feu (a beef-based broth cooked with carrots), and brandade de morue—a purée of salt codfish, milk or cream, olive oil, and crushed garlic—taking great pleasure in stretching his limited funds to buy the best and widest variety of foods Paris had to offer.

Starvation could easily destroy my concentration. My appetite's edge has become sharp, destructive. With only bread and margarine in his belly and not a sou in his pockets as he wandered the markets of Paris, George Orwell discovered the same sniveling self-pity that has overcome me. The world must have lost many writers and artists to hunger, people we've never heard of. Many so-called aspiring writers are merely enamored with the artistic life, but are doomed never to produce work of any significance to anyone, even to themselves. Orwell met a young man who lived with his mother in a boardinghouse. She darned socks for sixteen hours a day, every day, at twenty-five centimes per sock to support her son, who lounged about the cafés of Montparnasse, never knowing what starvation meant, nor the struggle that art demands. Whereas Langston Hughes arrived in Paris with barely a penny and found a way, quickly, to feed himself well, working as a busboy in a restaurant and living with a young Russian dancer in a cheap hotel. There they camped out on the single bed to consume feasts of bread and cheese and coarse red wine and pursued their art and waited for fame.

Writers living deprived lives produce better art, a Harvard administrator once told me as he puffed on his cigar and helped himself to another brandy. That morning he had denied a young writer her request for an important grant. He shares the common prejudice against commercially successful writers, as though the link between commerce and good writing can't exist, as though writers with money have somehow sold out. Why should writers make sacrifices while others feast and fatten off their work? Publishers have dined well on the profits of *Moby-Dick,* but in his lifetime, Herman Melville saw only a few good reviews and almost no sales of his great book. He wrote until he died, although he was unpublished in his last twenty years and worked to support his family as an outdoors customs inspector in downtown New York City. I have squandered more opportunities than he ever had. Perhaps the rich life is as destructive to the writer's imagination as extreme hunger. In his diary, Stendhal describes experiencing the lassitude of high society. I have lived too well, and perhaps, after all, I am blessed to have arrived here.

Bondage to hunger, when you can think about nothing else, forces compromise. Toward the end of his life, released from prison and living in exile on the Continent, Oscar Wilde charmed strangers to earn his keep, an act he had polished in better times, and yet, in his reduced and publicly shamed circumstances, the performance had a pathos to it that years earlier he would have scorned. In those last few years, Wilde called himself Sebastian Melmoth after *Melmoth the Wanderer,* a Gothic novel by his great-uncle. Melmoth sold his soul in exchange for a longer life, but was doomed to spend all his days seeking someone to relieve him from his contract with the Devil. Gone were the days when Wilde dined at the Café Royal in London, brilliantly entertaining his acolytes and colleagues and lovers while they dined on the Café's specialty, the entrecôtes.

"Imagine a poor exile," Twain wrote in *A Tramp Abroad.* He might as well have been talking about Wilde and me, sitting in our cells, writing.

> And imagine an angel suddenly sweeping down out of a better land and setting before him a mighty porterhouse steak an inch and a half thick, hot and sputtering from the griddle; dusted with fragrant pepper; enriched with little melting bits of butter of the most unimpeachable freshness and genuineness; and the precious juices of the meat trickling out and joining the gravy, archipelagoed with mushrooms; a township or two of tender, yellowish fat gracing an outlying district of this ample country of beefsteak;

the long white bone which divides the sirloin from the tenderloin still in its place; and imagine that an angel also adds a great cup of homemade American coffee, with the cream-a-froth on top, some real butter, firm and yellow and fresh, some smoking-hot biscuits, a plate of hot buckwheat cakes, with transparent syrup,—could words describe the gratitude of this exile?

When he traveled in Europe, Twain found Continental cookery pallid and unsubstantial, and he yearned for American food. He composed a wish list of the dishes he desired on his table, some sixty items, impossible to eat at one sitting, including baked apples with cream, fried chicken, southern style, and several types of bread and pastry.

If I can choose any company and any food I like for a literary meal in my cell, I might well start with some of Twain's robust, appetite-filling foods. Samuel Johnson once told James Boswell that "a hungry man has not the same pleasure in eating a plain dinner that a hungry man has in eating a luxurious dinner," and so I'll be extravagant, a gesture that at least one of my guests, Oscar Wilde, will appreciate.

• • •

I followed William Somerset Maugham to Asia, but I can't blame him for what has happened to me. He wrote about an opium dream in Singapore, but he was not arrested. Instead, tearooms in elegant Asian hotels have been named for him. He would pity me. "One of the most difficult things for a man to do is to realise that he does not stand at the center of things, but at the circumference," he wrote in *A Writer's Notebook*. I am at the center of my own little universe, and no one else is here.

Maugham wrote with distaste of his years without much money, of the distraction of financial worries, the unpleasantness of having to make do. "Hunger is a desire which is on the boundary line between pain and pleasure," he wrote. "It shows better than any other state that pain and pleasure arise from the degree of desire. When hunger is moderate the sensation is agreeable, and the idea of food gives pleasure; but when it is excessive there is only pain, and then one's thoughts are engaged not with the satisfactoriness of eating a good dinner, but merely with the getting rid of an unpleasant feeling." I am anticipating my plate of rice with impatience. I'll picture Mildred, the young waitress in *Of Human Bondage,* bringing me my next meal. Better yet, I'll picture Pomme, my voluptuous beauty, who will reveal Maugham's wisdom and will tell me, a little impatiently, that once I cease to live through my writers, then I'll begin to craft my own life, a connected life.

The meal in my cell with Maugham and Zola and Twain and Wilde and Crane will be the last frivolous time I spend in their company, my fond farewell celebration and formal thanks for everything they've taught me. When the meal is done, their stories told, they'll occupy a quieter place in my life. My pages will no longer tell the tales of the accomplishments of others. I'll use my deprivation, my time, and my solitude to write down the words I should have been writing all along. Hillaire Belloc once said, "Now that I have eaten a pheasant, drunk a bottle of Burgundy, and put away a cigar I can write in peace." Tomorrow, I will begin my novel.

• • •

THE FAREWELL FEAST

Brandade de Morue
Garlic Soup with Black Bread
Porterhouse Steak and Fried Potatoes
Baked Apples with Cream

--- ·~·꧁꧂·~· ---

1. BRANDADE DE MORUE
Adapted from *The Escoffier Cookbook* (the American edition of
Guide Culinaire, 1903), Auguste Escoffier

1 pound salt cod
1¼ cup plus 1 tablespoon extra-virgin olive oil
1 large clove garlic, crushed
½ cup milk
salt and pepper to taste
toast, cut into triangles

The day before preparing the brandade, soak the cod in cold water, changing the water every few hours to rinse off excess salt. Cover and let sit in water overnight in refrigerator.

Drain the fish and cut into chunks. Cover with water and bring to a boil and let poach for eight minutes. Drain the fish and remove all skin and bones.

In a saucepan heat ¼ cup plus 1 tablespoon olive oil until it smokes. Add fish and garlic and stir over medium-high heat until cod becomes a paste.

Remove from heat and add very gradually while stirring vigorously 1 cup oil alternating with ½ cup boiling milk. When done, the brandade will have the consistency of a potato purée. Adjust for seasoning. Serve with toast triangles.

Other recipes for brandade de morue vary the quantities of milk and oil. Others call for cream or crème fraîche instead of milk.

GARLIC SOUP
Adapted from *The Foods & Wines of Spain,* Penelope Casas, 1991

2 to 4 cloves garlic, peeled and crushed
4 slices bread, baguette style
3 tablespoons olive oil
4 cups chicken or beef broth or water
pinch saffron
1 tablespoon paprika
4 eggs (or one per person)

Preheat the oven to 450°F.

Sauté garlic and bread in olive oil until golden brown. Remove from oil and let oil cool.

Bring broth or water to boil in an ovenproof casserole. Add a pinch of saffron.

Stir 1 tablespoon paprika into oil. Add oil to broth. Add sautéed garlic and salt to taste. Cook for several minutes.

Crack 4 eggs into soup and place bread on top. Bake in oven for several minutes until eggs are set. Serve.

FRIED POTATOES
Adapted from *Larousse Gastronomique,* 1984

Peel, rinse, and cut new potatoes into thick slices. Pat dry and season with salt and pepper. Sauté uncovered in a mixture of butter and oil for 20–30 minutes. Cover when browned, stirring occasionally so that the potatoes finish cooking evenly.

BAKED APPLES
Adapted from *Modern Cookery for Private Families,* Eliza Acton, 1887

8 large apples, cored
8 curls of lemon peel, cut in strips
2 ounces candied orange peel or marmalade
1 cup soft pale brown sugar
1¼ cups muscatel or sweet white wine
granulated sugar

Run the point of a knife round the apple skins about two-thirds of the way up, to prevent them bursting. Stuff the cavities with mixture of lemon peel and orange peel or marmalade (dark marmalade with plenty of peel is best). Make a bed of the brown sugar in a baking dish. Place apples on top, and pour wine over the apples. Bake 35–45 minutes at 350–400°F as convenient. Remove when cooked, cool 5 minutes, then reshape with a spoon if necessary. Baste with the juices, sprinkle the tops with a close layer of granulated sugar, and grill until the apples acquire patchy black caps. Eat with cream immediately, or reheated later on, or when cold.

—◦◦⧼❧✦❧⧽◦◦—

CHAPTER SEVEN

Kitchen Arts

POMME'S SYLLABUS FOR AN
UNORTHODOX COOKING COURSE

When treasures are recipes they are less clearly, less distinctly remembered than when they are tangible objects. They evoke however quite as vivid a feeling—that is, to some of us who, considering an art, feel that a way of cooking can produce something that approaches an aesthetic emotion.

—Alice B. Toklas
The Alice B. Toklas Cookbook

As he chops, cuts, slices, trims, shapes, or threads through the string, a butcher is as good a sight to watch as a dancer or a mime. A Parisian butcher, that goes without saying.

—Colette
The Blue Lantern

What does cookery mean? It means the knowledge of Medea and of Circe, and of Calypso, and Sheba. . . . It means the economy of your great-grandmother and the science of modern chemistry, and French art, and Arabian hospitality. It means, in fine, that you are to see imperatively that everyone has something nice to eat.

—John Ruskin

*J*eremy once spent the better part of an evening instructing Pomme in music's superiority to all other arts. More precious because it is fleeting, more demanding in its practice, simply more important, he told her. Privately, Pomme disagreed with his argument, but because she loved Jeremy, she listened closely, raptly even. Later, after he broke her heart, she became suspicious of people who insist on the primacy of their own interests. She learned to distrust anyone who dismisses certain forms of creativity as less significant, less deserving of recognition, just plain *less.* She believes that cooking is an art, and now she challenges those who insist otherwise. She no longer takes her own abilities for granted.

In America, Pomme teaches a cooking course, a rigorous one that scatters dilettantes, one that elicits the full creative potential from her students. "Have you ever really understood what a cook was trying to accomplish with a meal?" Pomme asks the class in the first lesson. "Do you realize how many empty stomachs and greedy mouths are blind to a cook's creativity and passion? Have you properly acknowledged a chef's virtuoso performance? Or have you summoned a chef to your restaurant table merely to impress your friends with your worldly sophistication?" She is indignant that too many palates fail to perceive how a delicious meal is one cook's personal expression that might owe its inspiration to recipes left by the great nineteenth-century chef Carême or to the no-nonsense culinary techniques more recently taught by Julia Child, or to the artistry of another culinary mentor. "Shouldn't cooking be recognized as an art," Pomme asks her students, "a form of creative expression that demands perfection and an audience, that entertains and provokes us, that can shock or amuse us?"

Pomme assigns *Madame Bovary* and explains that Emma Bovary's wedding cake is called a *pièce montée,* an elaborately constructed dessert of the eighteenth and nineteenth centuries, when chefs looked to sculpture and architecture for inspiration. Faithful to Flaubert's description, the students bake and construct Emma's cake, a temple surrounded by statuettes with a turret made from gâteau de Savoie—a sponge lightened by the froth of many beaten egg whites—and fortifications composed of angelica, almonds, raisins, and orange segments. A layer representing a meadow crowns the cake, with boats of hazelnut shells floating on candied lakes and a tiny Cupid perched on a chocolate swing.[1] While the students whip egg whites and fuss over the precise placement of the hazelnut boats, Pomme reveals how cooking has also been compared to painting. She reads aloud a selection from W. H. Auden and Christopher Isherwood's *Journey to a War* praising the advanced culinary visual aesthetic of a Chinese meal served on the authors' Asian travels:

> One's first sight of a table prepared for a Chinese meal hardly suggests the idea of eating at all. It looks rather as if you were sitting down to a competition in water-color painting. The chopsticks, lying side by side, resemble paint-brushes. The paints are represented by little dishes of sauces, red, green, and brown. The tea-bowls, with their lids, might well contain paint-water. There is even a kind of tiny paint-rag, on which the chopsticks can be wiped. . . .
>
> Hors-d'oeuvre delicacies remain in presence throughout and this, too, is like painting; for the diners are perpetually mixing them in with their food to obtain varying combinations of taste.

She describes banquet rooms of medieval castles, in which servants paraded enormous pies before the diners, and then slashed open the crusts to release flocks of birds inside, creating a culinary theatrical performance. "Beyond obvious physical similarities to other arts, cooking is also an act of persuasion," she says. "By awakening your senses with good food, did the cook seduce you? When your tongue encountered jarring spices, or you suffered a raging thirst hours after a meal, had the cook intended deliberately to spite you? Was the combination of flavors so unusual that you could think only of the food at hand? Was the meal a Proustian one, evocative of pleasures past? For Proust a madeleine conjured the past, for Colette the aroma of charred chestnuts and of apples bubbling on the grate recalled tender moments in her personal history. Was their taste-memory akin to a musician's perfect pitch, as James Beard wrote? And if writers may endow food with symbolic meaning in literature, then might cooks also infuse their creations with rich significance, serving elegant ideas along with the meal?

"Don't you ever wonder how a confection as sweet as these almond tarts could make you mourn lost loves?" Pomme asks as the students blend lime juice with milk of almonds, true to the recipe from *Cyrano de Bergerac*. In the Bakery of the Poets, Cyrano learns of Roxanne's love for another man, the poets and pastry cooks blithely sing a recipe counterpoint to his breaking heart. It is a dish that Pomme has often made.

A RECIPE FOR MAKING ALMOND TARTS
Declaimed by the Pastry Cook, Ragueneau, in *Cyrano de Bergerac*, Edmond Rostand, 1898

> Beat your eggs, the yolk and white,
> Very light;
> Mingle with their creamy fluff
> Drops of lime juice, cool and green;
> Then pour in
> Milk of Almonds, just enough.

Dainty patty-pans, embraced
    In puff-paste—
Have these ready within reach;
    With your thumb and finger, pinch
    Half an inch
Up around the edge of each—

Into these, a score or more,
    Slowly pour
All your store of custard; so
    Take them, bake them golden-brown—
    Now sit down! . . .
Almond tartlets, Ragueneau!

The class reads Virginia Woolf's *To the Lighthouse* and prepares Mrs. Ramsay's boeuf en daube. The meat's exquisite scent of olives and oil and juice that provoked the scene's ardent mood accompany a lively class discussion about food and love. They move on to Graham Greene's story *Chagrin in Three Parts,* in which bouillabaisse and wine cast a mood between two women, making one of them ripe for seduction by the other. "Diners would do well to be alert when in the presence of the masters," Pomme says, awakening her students to the fullness of experience they've been missing at meals, shattering their previously held assumptions about cooking and art. "And if you believe that art and life are the same, then surely an essential part of artistic experience is that which nourishes it."

Pomme rarely allows her students to work from traditional recipes, relenting only when one might illuminate a detail of culinary history or method. Instead she urges her apprentices to discover through practice and thoughtful observation. A writer cannot create great works by writing to formula. Likewise, the best cooks are the ones who put something of themselves into the endeavor, not merely follow a set of instructions. Cooking and writing—for Pomme believes that of all the arts, these are the closest allies— when done with intent to achieve perfection, are demanding and very personal forms of work. A recipe might provide the basis for a meal, but every meal is singular, never to be exactly duplicated, influenced by things as mundane as the temperature gauge of the oven or the variation in the quality of the ingredients, and by nuances as subtle as personal interpretation of the recipe, refined through the individual's artistry and imagination. "That's why you will have trouble baking Emily Dickinson's Gingerbread," Pomme says as she hands out copies of the recipe written in the poet's own handwriting. The original may be found at Harvard among the papers of Emily's sister-in-law, Susan Huntington Gilbert Dickinson. Its glaze comes from a cookbook of the period, *Lyman's Philosophy of Housekeeping,* by a cousin of the Dickinson family, likely to have been kept in the Dickinson household.

EMILY DICKINSON'S GINGERBREAD
From *Emily Dickinson Face to Face,* Martha Dickinson Bianchi, 1932

1 Qt. Flour
½ cup Butter
½ cup Cream
½ Tablespoon Ginger
Salt
Make up with molasses

Cream the butter and mix with lightly whipped cream. Sift dry ingredients together and combine with other ingredients. The dough is stiff and needs to be pressed into whatever pan you choose. A round or small square pan is suitable. The recipe also fits perfectly into a cast iron muffin pan, if you happen to have one which makes oval cakes. Bake at 350° for 20–25 minutes.

To glaze or ice pastry—beat the yolk of an egg, and lay it on with a small brush or a bunch of feathers; or glaze with the whole egg beaten.

At the end of the recipe Susan had remarked, "But mine never tasted like hers."

While the students try their hand at Emily's culinary poetry, Pomme tells the story of MacGregor Jenkins, who lived as a child near the Dickinson family and later wrote a memoir that provides valuable clues about the gingerbread's taste and appearance. Emily often raided the pantry for Jenkins and his friends, hiding from her housekeeper as she stole food from the kitchen and lowered gingerbread-filled baskets from her window to the children waiting below. "It was not like any gingerbread I had ever seen before or have ever encountered since," Jenkins wrote. "It was in the form of long oval cakes, crisp and brown on the outside, but within light brown or yellow and delicately sweet or gummy. The flat tops were hard and shiny and there a bit of decoration was often added, in the way of a pansy or other small flower."

Emily's gingerbread is ultimately a lesson in humility, proof that a recipe can yield wildly extreme variations, many of them dry and surprisingly tasteless. Only Emily knew precisely how she made her gingerbread special, and food *was* special to her, a way to express love for the people she cared about. Pomme's attempt is fairly successful when she uses about a cup of molasses and four cups of flour, but Emily's recipe remains fickle and humbles her, reminding her never to feel arrogant about her art and yet always to strive for the best. What Pomme wants her students to understand is that whether one's choice of artistic expression lies in literature or cookery, there's no point in doing either unless the creation is the best possible, the most deeply satisfying experience first for the artist and then for others, the thrill of creation born as much from the process as from the result. The pleasure a cook takes in composing a soufflé that holds its delicate, airy form is akin to what a writer feels when he has written the perfect story, or novel, or poem, knowing that it's good, very good, and couldn't be made better.

Other artists have understood the cook, recognizing the similar demands in their crafts. Pomme's first lover in America, a writer and professor of English, admired her undaunted urge to create and the way she turns her sharp eye to find inspiration all about her. William Makepeace Thackeray compared the work of Alexis Soyer, the chef at London's Reform Club in the mid-nineteenth century, to poetry and cast him as a chef in one of his novels. "How finely it is written!" raved Thackeray in his review of Soyer's cookbook *The Gastronomic Regenerator* in 1846. "There is an account in the volume of crawfish aux truffes à la sampayo, which makes one almost frantic with hunger." In his preface, Soyer describes browsing the works of Milton, Locke, and Shakespeare in a great library when he encountered a cookbook. With false modesty, Soyer denied that his own culinary ideas should ever be worthy of a place in the Temple of the Muses. He urged his reader to place his simple publication "in a place suitable to its little merit, and not with Milton's sublime *Paradise,* for there it certainly would be doubly lost." A simple matter for Pomme's class to read between Soyer's lines to know that Soyer desired his cookbooks to be located precisely in the Pantheon, right *next* to Milton if possible. *The Times* review of February 19, 1847, said, "Like Byron, M. Soyer finds himself famous in the morning." How Soyer must have smiled.

Pomme knows how Byron would have sneered, insulted by being compared to the chef. Byron once crowed over the fate of a copy of Samuel Richardson's *Pamela,* the pages of which were used by an unsuspecting grocer to wrap flour and bacon for a gypsy woman wanted for murder. In his diary in 1821, Byron described Richardson as "the vainest and luckiest of living authors (i.e. while alive)—he who used to prophesy and chuckle over the presumed fall of Fielding (the prose Homer of human nature) and of Pope (the most beautiful of poets)—what would he have said, could he have traced his pages from their place on the French prince's toilets (see Boswell's Johnson) to the grocer's counter and the gipsy-murderer's bacon!!!"

Pomme teaches her apprentices to question assumptions and traditions—why salt and pepper are paired on Western tables when ginger used to be the essential seasoning, why we separate savory and sweet dishes when the flavors were once freely mixed, why we in the West eat three meals a day, why the idea of good taste measures not only our culinary sophistication but also our social status, why dessert comes last. She has the class prepare three essential medieval sauces: a yellow one based on ginger and saffron; another with ginger, cloves, cardamom, and green herbs; and one with the pretty name cameline, spiced with cinnamon and ginger. She has them cook entire meals in one pot, the way home cooks for centuries were obliged to cook over the fireplace before the invention of oven ranges. She sets one person in the class to baking a fine crusty white bread from wheat flour while the rest of the class bakes a strange-tasting pulse bread made from crushed peas, for hundreds of years the bread of the many poor of England who could not afford the precious grain flour. The history of cookery, Pomme reminds the students, like anything to do with humankind, comprises at least two stories—of the rich and the poor. While formal culinary arts evolved in Royal Courts and well-to-do European homes, the rest of Europe coped with potato famines, enclosure laws restricting general access to vital grazing land, punishing grain and salt taxes, and poaching regulations that carried penalties as stiff as deportation or even death.

She takes the class to a slaughterhouse where a butcher with massive scarred hands removes parts from a beef carcass. While he wreaks his damage on the beast with rapid and perfectly placed cuts, Pomme explains how some meats were once considered suitable only for servants, and how the Smithfield slaughterhouse in Victorian London attracted members of the upper classes who drank fresh blood to prevent tuberculosis. Later in the course, Pomme invites the students to her home in the country where they select chickens from Pomme's own roost to wring their necks, pluck the feathers, and singe the down to prepare the birds for cooking. Every serious cook should experience an act like this at least once in order to understand the basic methods of our art, she tells the students. Pomme shocks the more squeamish among the students with her story of Asian poultry merchants who bite out the tongues from live birds' throats, the tongue being a delicacy that fetches excellent prices. So that they'll understand the seriousness of their undertaking, Pomme also tells them the story of chef Vatel.

On April 26, 1671, Madame de Sévigné wrote a letter about the royal chef Vatel, who despaired at the imagined loss of his reputation when two tables went short of roast meat during the King's supper. A personal visit from the Prince himself could not console him. The next morning at four, Vatel supervised a delivery of fish. He had ordered fish from all seaports in the vicinity, yet only one purveyor had arrived. "Vatel waited for some time," Madame de Sévigné wrote, "his head grew distracted; he thought there was no more fish to be had." Unable to bear the disgrace of producing a second incomplete meal, Vatel returned to his apartment "and setting the hilt of his sword against the door, after two ineffectual attempts, succeeded in the third, in forcing the sword through his heart. At that instant the carriers arrived with the fish; Vatel was inquired after to distribute it; they ran to his apartment, knocked at the door, but received no answer; upon which they broke it open, and found him weltering in his own blood."

No matter how seriously you take your art, Pomme tells her students as she wrings a bird's neck, don't panic if a meal has not turned out right. A culinary disaster is rarely, if ever, worth dying over.

Which brings Pomme to a discussion of the Culinary Canon. Predictably, her students have heard of François Pierre de la Varenne, Fanny Farmer, and Auguste Escoffier, but are uncertain of their contributions to modern cookery. They are even less familiar with Antonin Carême, Hannah Glasse, Maria Rundell, Isabella Beeton, Eliza Acton. The class prepares one of each cook's dishes to learn how foods and cooking styles have changed over centuries and to understand the sources of modern tastes and technique. Period literature lays the proper social setting for each class meal: Molière, La Fontaine, and De Sévigné accompany their preparation of the food of La Varenne; Jonathan Swift and Alexander Pope if the recipes are by Hannah Glasse; Stendhal, Balzac, and Dumas, père if Carême is at table; the Trollopes, Flaubert, George Sand, and the Goncourts for Escoffier.

Twenty years before Vatel's suicide, a French court chef named François Pierre de la Varenne wrote *Le Cuisinier françois,* the first cookbook that called for delicate seasonings, for roasts served in their own natural juices finished off with simple sauces based on meat drippings, for butter instead of oil or meat fats in pastries, including recipes for familiar dishes such as puff paste, petit fours, bouquets garnis, cream soups, and basic bouillon. Another innovation—the cookbook was arranged alphabetically. *Le Cuisinier françois,* with early editions in English and Italian, announced the transition from a style of cooking that had exploited spices and other flavorings to mask rather than to enhance a food's natural flavors. After praising the contributions of court cooks like La Varenne, Pomme cautions the class never to forget the home cook. *The Art of Cookery Made Plain and Easy, Which Far Exceeds Anything of the Kind Yet Published,* by A Lady, addressed the household cook rather than cooks at court and reveals the best of English home cooking from breads and pies to pickles and preserves to home-brewed wines and liqueurs. Published in 1747 when the author was twenty-three years old—she had eloped at age sixteen—the book went through more than twenty printings in fifty years. Throughout the hundreds of recipes in the book, the lady's style is conversational, her instructions are blessedly simple, and most of her recipes are easy to prepare, like her lemon cream.

LEMON CREAM

Take the juice of five large lemons, half a pint of water, a pound of double-refined sugar beaten fine, the whites of seven eggs, and the yolk of one beaten very well, mix all together, strain it, and set it on a gentle fire, stirring all the while, and scum it clean, put into it the peel of one lemon, when it is very hot, but don't boil, take out the lemon-peel, and pour it into china dishes. You must observe to keep it stirring one way all the time it is over the fire.

Samuel Johnson and bookstore owners Edward and Charles Dilly disputed the gender of the author of *The Art of Cookery.* Surely a man wrote the book, they insisted. A woman could have never produced such an excellent work, Johnson said, declaring his own intentions to compile a cookbook. According to Anne Willan in *Great Cooks and Their Recipes,* it was not until the twentieth century that a local historian discovered Hannah Glasse's identity.

When poet Eliza Acton brought her work to a publisher, he said he'd prefer that she write a cookbook. Perhaps I'm making an unfair comparison, Pomme tells the class, but what if a young John Updike had been told to give up fiction and to write a homeowner's carpentry guide instead? Acton teased her publishers about their cupidity in *Modern Cookery for Private Families,* published in 1845. Her Poor-Author's Pudding calls for milk, bread, and a little sugar, while her recipe for Publisher's Pudding "can scarcely be made too rich" and boasts lavish quantities of almonds, cream, butter, marrow, and brandy.[2]

"When both the mind and body are exhausted by the toils of the day, heavy or unsuitable food, so far from recruiting their enfeebled powers, prostrates their energies more completely, and acts in every way injuriously upon the system." So Acton set out to teach the inexperienced cook about food, something she said no other cookbook had ever accomplished. Acton claimed to be the first to establish uniform measurements and cooking times, and among the first to present cookery as both accessible and enjoyable.

With Glasse and Acton concerned about practical home cookery, Auguste Escoffier, a chef to Napoleon III as well as the first chef of the Savoy Hotel in London in the late 1800s, practiced his art on high society. While Escoffier concerned himself with honest cuisine, his shady practices in the kitchen nearly led to his arrest. At the Savoy, he confessed to committing larceny in a scheme to resell inventory. The hotel chose not to press charges against its renowned founding chef. *Le Guide Culinaire,* published in 1902, became an essential guide to classic cuisine bearing Escoffier's stamp of simplicity—both in the diminished number of dishes brought to table in one meal and in the reduced variety of flavors at one sitting. Above all, he said, intimate meals require the greatest finesse and quality, the desired atmosphere of any dining occasion as essential as the menu itself. He warned readers not to make the dreadful faux pas of serving a dish named for a famous courtesan in the company of her rival, but to be always attuned to the spirit of the diners to achieve a fully orchestrated occasion.

As Pomme teaches the essential techniques of the Western world's great cooks, she clarifies the influences of other cultures on their art, how Eastern spices like ginger and cinnamon and sugar are the parents of Western cookery, how imports like chocolate and salt transformed the kitchens of Europe. She shows the class how fearlessness leads to innovation, how a classic French recipe might after all be improved with a hint of lemon grass from Thailand, how there is no one right way to do these things.

She cautions them to beware the deconstructionists who try to strip the joy from cooking and eating. Roland Barthes studied the semiotic content of cookery columns found in *Elle* and *L'Express* magazines. Claude Lévi-Strauss decoded a meal in "The Raw and the Cooked." Nutritionists break recipes down into statistics concerning fat content and nutritional value. Pomme has room for none of them in her class.

Like any of the arts, cooking explores the senses, and Pomme wants to wake them up, have the students see, taste, and understand food for the first time, to learn when yeast is proved and fresh bread baked by their scent and never by the sound of a kitchen timer, to taste when the complicated flavors of certain spices are perfectly balanced, to feel egg whites froth up under the strength of their own hands and a whisk—not a high-speed blender's blade— to watch and wait for the precise moment when a batch of sugar candy has balled to the right temperature or when a sauce has sufficiently thickened. Pomme urges the students to experiment with their cooking styles, to be bold and brave—the way writers strike out to test their style, tone, and subject—to develop their instincts and knowledge into personal forms of culinary expression. All along the way, Pomme has her students write down what they experience, to force their thoughts onto a page. Otherwise their time in her kitchen might well be transient, passing too quickly before being properly considered and understood. Pomme is singularly determined to transform the dailiness of cooking and eating into something sublime in the hearts and minds of all who come near her.

The students work hard for Pomme, and their artistry will mature with repetition and ritual, becoming flawless after years of constant application. Near the end of the course, Pomme gives her students a gift, a copy of *Le Répertoire de la Cuisine,* a staple in her own kitchen, a reference to standard recipes and the foundation for her own interpretations. Learning to use this book frees the students from all other cookbooks. Their final exam is to prepare a meal of the five dishes they consider essential in their repertoire. Pomme looks for imagination and spirit, boldness and clarity of vision, knowledge of ingredients, presentation and taste.

At the end of Pomme's course, over a feast that the class prepares, Pomme tells the story of Jeremy, the musician she once loved and how he had been wrong. No art can claim a superior position over the others, she explains. Room for creative expression exists in any field of endeavor. In the end, she says, Proust described creativity in the kitchen best when he recalled a luncheon at Combray:

> And when all these had been eaten, a work composed expressly for ourselves, but dedicated more particularly to my father who had a fondness for such things—a cream of chocolate, inspired in the mind, created by the hand of

Françoise, would be laid before us, light and fleeting as a piece of music, into which she had poured the whole of her talent. Anyone who refused to partake of it, saying: "No, thank you, I have finished, I am not hungry," would have at once been lowered to the level of the Philistines who, when an artist makes them a present of one of his works, examines its weight and material, whereas what is of value is the creator's intention and his signature. To have left even the tiniest morsel in the dish would have shown as much discourtesy as to rise and leave a concert hall while the piece was still being played, and under the composer's very eyes.[3]

----

1 . SAVOY CAKE

There are two kinds of Savoy cake. The gâteau de Savoie is made from brioche dough and filled with pralines. The biscuit de Savoie is a sponge cake that calls for 14 eggs for every 2¼ cups of sugar.

2 . THE PUBLISHER'S PUDDING
From *Modern Cookery for Private Families,* Eliza Acton, 1887

This pudding can scarcely be made *too rich*. First blanch, and then beat to the smoothest possible paste, six ounces of fresh Jordan almonds, and a dozen bitter ones; pour very gradually to them, in the mortar, three quarters of a pint of boiling cream; then turn them into a cloth and wring from them again with strong expression. Heat a full pint of it afresh, and pour it, as soon as it boils, upon four ounces of fine bread-crumbs, set a plate over, and leave them to become nearly cold; then mix thoroughly with them four ounces of macaroons, crushed tolerably small; five of finely minced beef-suet, five of marrow, cleared very carefully from fibre, and from the splinters of bone which are sometimes found in it, and shred not very small, two ounces of flour, six of pounded sugar, four of dried cherries, four of the best Muscatel raisins, weighed after they are stoned, half a pound of candied citron, or of citron and orange rind mixed, a quarter saltspoonful of salt, half a nutmeg, the yolks only of seven full-sized eggs, the grated rind of a large lemon, and last of all, a glass of the best Cognac brandy, which must be stirred briskly in by slow degrees. Pour the mixture into a thickly buttered mould or basin, which contains a full quart, fill it to the brim, lay a sheet of buttered writing-paper over, then a well-floured cloth, tie them securely, and boil the pudding for four hours and a quarter; let it stand for two minutes before it is turned out; dish it careful; and serve it with the German pudding-sauce [see below].

A GERMAN CUSTARD PUDDING SAUCE
From *Modern Cookery for Private Families,* Eliza Acton, 1887

Boil very gently together half a pint of new milk or of milk and cream mixed, a very thin strip or two of fresh lemon-rind, a bit of cinnamon, half an inch of a vanilla bean, and an ounce and a half or two ounces of sugar, until the milk is strongly flavored; then strain, and pour it, by slow degrees, to the well-beaten yolks of three eggs, smoothly mixed with a *knife-end-full* (about half a teaspoonful) of flour, a grain or two of salt, and a tablespoonful of cold milk; and stir these very quickly round as the milk is added. Put the sauce again into the stewpan, and whisk or stir it rapidly until it thickens, and looks creamy. It must not be placed *upon* the fire, but should be held over it, when this is done. The Germans *mill* their sauces to a froth; but they may be whisked with almost equally good effect, though a small mill for the purpose—formed like a chocolate mill—may be had at a very trifling cost.

3 . CREAM OF CHOCOLATE
Adapted from *The Household Cookery Book,* Félix Urbain-Dubois, 1871

Prepare three-quarters of a mould-ful of cream with vanilla [see below]; when thickened, let it half-cook, agitating it.

Dissolve half a pound of chocolate, in a stewpan, at the entrance of the oven; first bray it with a spoon, then gradually dilute it with the cream; now add to the preparation 5 ounces of dissolved "gelatin," stir it on ice for a few minutes only. Then immediately pour it into a mould, embedded in ice.

When about to serve, dip the mould in warm water, turn the cream out on a cold dish.

VANILLA CREAM
Adapted from *The Household Cookery Book,* Félix Urbain-Dubois, 1871

Bray in a stewpan 6 yolks of eggs, add to them 9 ounces of powder-sugar; dilute the preparation with a pint and a half of milk, stir it on the fire, without leaving it, so as to prevent any ebullition. A few moments previous to taking the cream off the fire, add to it some vanilla; as soon as the cream is thickened to the degree requisite, pour it into a kitchen-basin, passing it through a sieve.

This cream may be served, either cold or warm; it may be perfumed, either with lemon-zest, or orange blossoms, or else with orange-zest.

CHOCOLATE CREAM
Adapted from *Dining with Proust,* Jean-Bernard Naudin, Anne Borrel, Alain Senderens, 1992

1 pint milk
4 ounces semisweet chocolate, broken in pieces
6 egg yolks
½ cup sugar

Preheat oven to 250°F.
Beat egg yolks with sugar.
Bring milk to a boil. Add chocolate and stir over low heat until chocolate is melted.
Remove from heat, pour chocolate over the egg and sugar mixture, and stir vigorously.
Strain the chocolate cream and pour into ramekins. Cook in a bain-marie for one hour. Cool and serve.

CHAPTER EIGHT

The Wages of Greed

I've not thought about Pomme in ages. After I broke off our affair, telling her the easy lie that I'd fallen for another woman, she kept appearing at unexpected moments. I'd notice her at the end of my street when I left for rehearsals, or in the restaurant where I meet my reading group every two weeks. She'd just sit there—always alone—until she saw that I'd noticed her. Then she'd suddenly leave without saying a word. She spooked me, killing my appetite for the food and the books. (We had been reading Rabelais.)

Several weeks after she stopped showing up at the restaurant, she invited me to her home. She wanted to prepare a fine dinner as a gesture of rapprochement, as she put it. She had planned a meal based on a novel I admire, *Nana,* by Émile Zola, in which the courtesan Nana serves a banquet to show off her wealth. Pomme's invitation tempted me. She knew I'd be easily seduced by the thought of such a meal, extravagant by any literary and culinary standards. Brebant's, a Parisian restaurant popular with writers because the proprietor ran a tab, supplied the food for Nana: thick asparagus soup à la Comtesse, clear soup à la Deslignac, rissoles of young rabbit with truffles, gnocchis and Parmesan cheese, carp à la Chambourd, saddle of venison à l'Anglaise, pullets à la maréchale, sole with shallot sauce, and Strasbourg pâté all washed down with Meursault, Chambertin, and Léoville, followed by cèpes à l'Italienne, pineapple fritters à la Pompadour,[1] and coffee. I accepted Pomme's invitation immediately.

On the day of Pomme's dinner, I glanced at the scene in *Nana* to ready an appropriate bon mot or two for our conversation. How could I have forgotten the disastrous outcome of Zola's meal, where the guests sweltered in the crowded heat, where "hunger was of the nervous order only, a mere whimsical craving born of an exasperated stomach," where an old whore indulged herself and then felt stupid at the thought of having overeaten, and where a host of new jealousies and alliances formed at various intoxicated stages of the evening?

I decided to forgo Pomme's invitation—clearly she had conceived a disturbing evening for me. I prepared a small supper for myself, a restrained meal that Byron himself preferred when he was in Ravenna—"mashed potatoes mixed with butter and aromatic herbs from the pine woods beyond the beaches, lapped in béchamel sauce, thickly powdered with grated cheese, and finished in the oven."[2] Then I went out of town. When I returned, I found complaining messages that Pomme had slipped under my door, each note angrier than its predecessor, going on about the wasted dinner, how rude could I be, how hateful, etc., etc. I never replied, and although I felt a tiny twinge of guilt, at least she stopped harassing me. Soon after, she went to Paris and then moved to America. I've not seen her in a couple of years.

The other morning I prepared myself some toast. "What can it be, that subtle treachery that lurks in tea-cakes, and is totally absent in the rude honesty of toast?" John Ruskin once said, giving me courage to resist the piece of cake leftover from yesterday's dessert. I was in one of my Byronic moods. I wanted a simple repast, like the tea and dried biscuits that the poet lived on for days at a time, denying the flesh, starving out temptation while he concentrated on his art. My self-control is not so sure, and I craved some jam for the toast. True, I've put on a little weight recently, but a touch of jam would not harm. I reached into the cupboard to find, hidden at the very back, five jars of redcurrant jam with labels in Pomme's handwriting, each inscribed with a literary reference or else a suggestion about how to serve the jam. "Take it as the French do," read the first label, "a dollop plain on your plate for a sweet dessert, perhaps mixed with cream cheese. Or spread some with fresh country butter on bread or toast with your morning tea and eat it, moodily, contemplatively, thinking about your music, about your life, about me. All my love." Pomme indulged my fondness for rich, sweet foods. She often baked a gâteau au fromage de Brie for me, a cake made from Brie cheese and butter, a recipe by Alexandre Dumas,[3] whose cookbook I keep by my bedside for occasional reading. A quotation from Samuel Johnson accompanied Pomme's instructions: "For my part, I mind my belly most studiously and very carefully; for I look upon it that he who does not mind his belly will hardly mind anything else."

But is Pomme comparing me to Johnson, a ravenous man who once devoured a hare that had been kept far too long and meat pies made of rancid butter, gorging himself with such violence that the veins in his forehead swelled almost to bursting? The second jar read, "Better to die of good wine and good company than of slow disease and doctors' doses," Thackeray's justification for the pleasures of indulgence.

The jars must have been sitting for at least two years, and yet they were perfectly sealed. The jam tastes delicious. I have taken Pomme's advice to eat it plain and I am sitting by the window, watching my little corner of London, as I write in my journal. How odd to have Pomme in mind again. In three days I have fully consumed two pots of jam, which are, after all, on the small side. I devour one quite happily as I write my early morning entry.

• • •

Balzac said that a woman is a well-served table that one sees with different eyes after the meal, a comment that reminds me of Pomme's cloying company. I could not take her in too great a quantity nor too frequently. When I fell for her blandishments and insistent ways, I felt glutted, overly full and uncomfortable. After we made love, she would sometimes recite passages from Colette. In retaliation, I'd read selections from Byron's letters, to which she'd listen carefully but with a petulant frown. "I wish to God I had not dined now!" he wrote. "It kills me with heaviness, stupor, and horrible dreams;—and yet it was but a pint of bucellas, and fish. Meat I never touch,—nor much vegetable diet. I wish I were in the country, to take exercise,—instead of being obliged to cool by abstinence, in lieu of it. I should not so much mind a little accession of the flesh,—my bones can well bear it. But the worst is, the devil always comes with it,—till I starve him out,—and I will not be the slave of any appetite." I will not be the slave of any appetite. I used to read that line to Pomme with a touch of menace in my voice and a certain emphasis on the word *any*. Pomme came to hate everything that Byron represented, myself included.

After these little readings, our form of literary warfare in which my heroes stood ground as sworn enemies against Colette, Pomme usually left me alone. When the door slammed behind her, I realized what Rilke meant when he said that artistic experience lies so incredibly close to the pain and ecstasy of sex. After I had finished with Pomme, I desired only to create that burning excitement in my music and avoid the look of unspoken accusation in her eyes that I had, once again, rejected her.

My stomach has been giving me trouble again. I thought a simple breakfast of toast would soothe me and restore my energy. The label on the jam read, "The physical pleasure which a certain woman gives you at a certain moment, the exquisite dish which you ate on a certain day—you will never meet either again. Nothing is repeated, and everything is unparalleled." At first the reference puzzled me, as Pomme had omitted the source, but I soon recognized the unmistakable style. A quick check in the Goncourt diary confirmed my instinct and corroborated my own conviction that no experience lives up to our ideals about what life should be like. One's expectations are rarely met. Several days before I broke with Pomme, I read that same passage in the Goncourt diary and the words spurred me to action as though written just for me. I knew then that I had to leave her. Pomme had been trying to capture and preserve our affair, to crystalize its earliest, most exciting stages. For me, boredom had predictably closed in, but letting go of Pomme has also coincided with a kind of letting go of myself. My search for novel, thrilling experiences has become relentless. I take risks, but lately, on several occasions, I've lost control to the point of collapse. I set out for an evening's entertainment and find myself in the morning at some strange hotel surrounded by the remains of a feast, an anonymous lover in the bed beside me who has drained me of all my creative energy. The Goncourts describe my life well. In November 1852 they wrote:

> We are supping out a great deal this year: mad suppers where they served mulled wine made from Léoville and peaches à la Condé[4] costing 72 francs the dish, in the company of trollops picked up at Mabille and shopsoiled sluts who nibble at these feasts with a bit of the sausage they had for dinner stuck in their teeth. One of them once exclaimed

naively: "Why, it's four o'clock . . . Ma's just peeling her carrots." We made them drunk and strip the animal that lives inside a silk dress.

I always seek the animal in the silk dress, nor can I deny the animal in myself. After my indulgences, I reach the lowest ebb in my work.

My mind and spirit are clear when I live a clean and simple, conventionally moral life. When I'm working on a new composition and experience the familiar urges, I concoct a restorative that Charles Baudelaire drank to help him through his own crises, a substitute for stimulants to keep his mind focused on his work. Found under the heading "Hygiene, Conduct, Morality" in his diary, the drink has proved an effective appetite killer. The taste is foul. I drink it down in deep gulps, holding my breath.

Fish, cold baths, showers, moss, pastilles occasionally, together with the abstinence from all stimulants. Iceland moss . . . 125 grammes. White sugar . . . 250 grammes. Soak the moss for twelve to fifteen hours in a sufficient quantity of cold water, then pour off the water. Boil the moss in two liters of water upon a slow and constant fire until these two liters are reduced to one, skim the froth off once, then add the 250 grammes of sugar and let it thicken to the consistency of syrup. Let it cool off. Take three very large spoonfuls daily, in the morning, at midnight, and in the evening. One need not be afraid to increase the doses if the crises are too frequent.

Naturally, the kind of sweet I prefer on my tongue is something like this redcurrant jam, but for the sake of my art, I must on occasion firmly deny the flesh. I need a glass of Baudelaire's elixir today. My stomach cramps persist and I'm feeling faint.

Sometimes I wonder if the deprivation I suffered as a child compels me to overindulge myself. Forced to work in a factory at age twelve and often hungry, did Charles Dickens fill his novels with food to compensate for his own days of starvation and lack of family comforts? One critic of Dickens pointed out that *The Pickwick Papers* boasts eighty-five meals. Yet in his life, Dickens tended to be abstemious rather than gluttonous.

Writers who lived indulgently yet managed also to produce important, or at least notable, work suffered for their behavior. I think about James Boswell, who, on the evening of January 12, 1763, took Louisa, a woman he had been trying to seduce for months, to an inn under a false name:

> At last my charming companion appeared, and I immediately conducted her to a hackney-coach which I had ready waiting, pulled up the blinds, and away we drove to the destined scene of delight. We contrived to seem as if we had come off a journey, and carried in a bundle our night-clothes, handkerchiefs, and other little things. We also had with us some almond biscuits, or as they call them in London, macaroons,[5] which looked like provision on the road. On our arrival at Haywards's we were shown into the parlour, in the same manner that any decent couple would be. I here thought proper to conceal my own name (which the people of the house had never heard), and assumed the name of Mr. Digges. . . . That Ceres and Bacchus might in moderation lend their assistance to Venus, I ordered a gentell supper and some wine.

Six days later, poor Bozzy came down with the clap. Hoping to confirm or remove his suspicions about the infection—he thought he felt its prickly heat coming on but could not be certain—he spent a day in vigorous exercise, walking across London with friends, "joined with hearty eating and drinking." Perhaps his pockets were filled with gingerbread and apples, as was the custom. They stopped in a public house "and drank some warm white wine with aromatic spices, pepper and cinnamon." Boswell spent considerable time and money on his recovery. He cut Louisa out of his life, abruptly, cleanly, justly.

Exquisite pleasure is often punished. This thought in mind, I seek the clubby company of my friends, who never criticize my manners at the table or my decision to have a third helping of dessert—which can sometimes be more desirable than helping yourself to the woman you're dining with. (Who else but a woman—Fanny Trollope—could have written a book called *Domestic Manners of the Americans,* condemning the eating habits of an entire nation?) I'll also call on my friends for a Byronic meal. Of an 1813 dinner with Byron and the banker and patron of the arts Samuel Rogers, Thomas Moore wrote that "Lord Byron, who, according to his frequent customs, had not dined for the last two days, found his hunger no longer governable, and called aloud for 'something to eat.' Our repast,—of his own choosing,—was simple bread and cheese; and seldom have I partaken of so joyous a supper." The three men spent the evening reading aloud and mocking the poetry of a contemporary, inferior poet, a riotous occasion I'd love to have shared.

Admittedly, Byron had strange manners. The first time he ate at Rogers's he refused any food save potatoes mashed with vinegar, but later went on to his club where he ate beefsteaks. "Byron had prodigious facility of composition," said Rogers. "He was fond of suppers; and used often to sup at my house and eat heartily (for he had given up the hard biscuit and soda-water diet); after going home, he would throw off sixty or eighty verses, which he would

send to press next morning." Byron's biographer suggested, somewhat spitefully, that Byron put up with Rogers for the sake of a
good meal. Others hinted that Rogers, an older man, naturally fell
for the charms of the younger, who was noted for his nobility,
beauty, and gentle voice. Later Byron turned on Rogers, harshly,
writing a satiric poem about a banker whose chief characteristic is
envy and whose one accomplishment is a single poem. Rogers's
poetry spoke to a small audience. The critics scorned his "Ode to
a Gnat."

Byron, so sensible, preferred not to dine with women, knowing, I'm sure, their potentially destructive effect on a finely wrought
artistic temperament. One of his lovers, Caroline Lamb, wrote in
her diary that he was "mad—bad—and dangerous to know"; she
provoked embarrassing scenes in public, even sending him token
clippings of her publc hair. (Thank God I never told Pomme about
Miss Lamb.) No wonder he refused female company from time to
time, preserving his energy for something more productive than an
overattentive, jealous woman who perceived the slightest reluctance
on his part as a challenge, a call to amatory arms. There must have
been nothing more enjoyable than to join Byron at his club to dine
on lobsters—two or three apiece—with strong white brandy alternating with tumblers of very hot water to aid our digestion. After
that, we'd have claret, easily dispatching two bottles between us, or
perhaps a Regency punch—"composed of Madeira, brandy, and
green tea, no real water being admitted therein"—talking all the
while, not parting until four o'clock in the morning, oblivious to the
lateness of the hour.[6] I cannot think of one female writer in whose
company I would want to spend such a time—most particularly and
most emphatically not Colette. The thought of that woman is making my stomach churn.

I don't think I'll be going out tonight with these cramps in my gut. I'm feeling listless and I've been sweating heavily. I really should start to take some exercise.

• • •

"If you don't like your victuals, pass on to the next article; but remember that every man who has been worth a fig in this world, as poet, painter, or musician, has had a good appetite and a good taste," reads the label on the fourth jar of jam. At first I thought Pomme meant to flatter me with this message. Then I realized that she has again insulted me. Thackeray wrote those words about Byron. His sentiment continued, jealously and unjustly. "Ah, what a poet Byron would have been had he taken his meals properly, and allowed himself to grow fat—if nature intended him to grow fat—and not have physicked his intellect with wretched opium pills and acrid vinegar, that sent his principles to sleep, and turned his feelings sour! If that man had respected his dinner, he never would have written Don Juan." Byron became the immortal poet I admire precisely because he *did* respect his dinner. He knew precisely the complicated effects of food on his delicate system and understood how to preserve the correct frame of his mind and body in order to create. I hope I might also achieve that exquisite balance between appetite and restraint to enhance my natural creative abilities, something Thackeray never knew. John Ruskin once observed that "Thackeray settled like a meat-fly on whatever one had for dinner, and made one sick of it." Indeed, how can you take a man seriously who preferred grilled cheese on toast to all other food?

In my endeavor at moderation, I am resisting the idea of devouring the fifth pot of jam until I have finished my new composition. Though I'm inclined to ravish it merely to get it out of the way. The jam has provoked uneasy thoughts of Pomme, a constant, sharp unsettlement in my mind. I had forgotten the unpleasant side effects of the dark and deceptively lovely Pomme.

Pomme often accused me of being cold, of living in the past, of preferring a fine glass of claret and a juicy steak to her company, although that didn't prevent her from craving my presence. When I'm in a mood of focused creativity, nothing can pierce my concentration and Pomme merely became a nuisance. At times like that, I wanted only to offend and chase her away, to tell her that Byron was right, that the women in Venice do kiss far better than any others, herself included. Balzac had the right idea by choosing a woman, Madame Hanska, who lived thousands of miles away in Russia, leaving him time to create brilliant works and to indulge his appetites, as his biographer Léon Gozlan described:

> The fruit that he kept on the table was astonishingly beautiful and savory. His lips quivered, his eyes shone with pleasure, his hands trembled, at the sight of a heap of pears, of luscious peaches. Not one would remain to tell of the annihilation of the others. He devoured them all. He was superb at the vegetarian Pantagruelism.

Balzac kept to a strict, admirable writing schedule and ate little when in the throes of creation: Bed at 8:00 P.M. after a light dinner and a glass or two of wine. Back to his writing desk by 2:00 A.M. until 6:00, all the time drinking coffee from a pot kept on the fire. Bath at 6:00 A.M., when the servant brought more coffee. From 9:00 A.M. he worked until noon, dining then on two boiled eggs and bread. The afternoon hours between 1:00 and 6:00 were taken up with revisions. He lived this spartan existence for weeks or months at a time. Unleashed from the routine, he erupted in bursts of indulgence, on one occasion stuffing himself on macaroni pies and rice cakes in a Paris bakery as though he had never eaten in his life.[7]

Zola too had a passion for cakes and ate entire platefuls with his tea. Edmond de Goncourt asked him once if he considered himself a glutton. "Yes," Zola replied, "it's my only vice; and at home, when there isn't anything good for dinner, I'm miserable, utterly miserable. That's the only thing that matters; nothing else really exists for me. You know what my life is like?" In the end, food was all that mattered to him. Sometimes I think that should be enough.

Like Byron, I have trouble harnessing my moments of abandon and fall prey to the same horrors of digestion that he felt upon overeating. I attempt to hide my excesses from myself, understanding what he meant when he said that "a true voluptuary will never abandon his mind to the grossness of reality. It is by exalting the earthly, the material, the physique of our pleasures, by veiling these ideas, by forgetting them altogether, or, at least, never naming them hardly to one's self, that we alone can prevent them from disgusting."

When I lie in my bed at night, gripping my stomach with its relentless stabbing pains, I make false promises, reminding myself to eat less, to chew each mouthful more slowly and deliberately, to concentrate my energy on my work. Henry James once suffered stomach crises like this, the result of Fletcherism, named for nutritionist Horace Fletcher, who advised his devotees to chew every mouthful one hundred times. For five years, James dutifully chewed his food fifty times on each side of his mouth until the whole idea of eating repulsed him, so laborious was every meal. No, Fletcherism will not be my route to self-control.

Briefly I considered a vegetarian diet, like Shelley and Shaw and Tolstoy. "Any man of my spiritual intensity does not eat corpses," Shaw once said, but H. G. Wells caught him in his lie—"he takes liver extract and calls it 'those chemicals.'" Shelley produced admirable work in many languages, including a treatise on vegetarianism, but his life of turmoil—complicated affairs with neurotic women, quarrels with his father, the deaths or estrangement of his children, culminating in his own death by drowning at thirty—hardly recommends a vegan's course to me. The foods available to a vegetarian—like the salad Aphrodite that Pomme prepared for me once—are merely dressed in elegant names to cloak insipid taste.[8]

Something is eating my soul, consuming me from inside out. I'm not usually so restless, so feverish. I am nauseated. My skin is clammy and grey, my sweats are heavier. I imagine that I'm feeling the punishing effects of recent nights when I consumed too many red meats and red wines and rich desserts. Tomorrow I will take a spartan diet of toast, perhaps taken with the last of the jam.

• • •

Pomme has truly baffled me. The label on the last jar reads: "Flaubert dined profitably and controversially on this." I cannot recall a single instance of Flaubert consuming jam. As I eat from the pot with a little toast on the side and a cup of strong tea, I feel a lassitude that prevents me from doing little more than writing slowly and remaining still.

What is the meaning of this jam? Balzac once tasted hashish jam at the Club des Haschischins and described his impressions in a letter to Madame Hanska, saying: "I heard celestial voices and saw divine pictures. It took me twenty years to descend Lauzun's staircase. I saw the gilding and the paintings in the drawing-room bathed in an indescribable splendour. But this morning, ever since waking, I am half-asleep, still and without the strength of will to do anything." The doctor who supplied the hashish was experimenting with the drug's effects for possible medical use. He recruited artists and writers—including the poet and novelist Théophile Gautier—to provide reliable reports of their hashish experiences. Gautier described one of the soirées in *The Hashish Club:*

> Thumb-sized morsels of greenish paste of jam had been scooped from a crystal dish with a spatula and set on each saucer beside a vermeil spoon. The doctor's face beamed with enthusiasm; his eyes sparkled; his cheeks were deeply flushed; the veins stood out on his temples; his dilated nostrils drew in air greedily. "This shall be deducted from your share of paradise," he said as he handed me my dose. When everyone had eaten his portion, coffee was served in the Arabian manner, that is, with the grounds and without sugar. We then took our places at table. This reversal of normal culinary practice has no doubt surprised the reader; indeed it is not at all customary to take coffee before soup, and jam is generally eaten as dessert.
>
> As the dinner came to an end, some of the more fervent adepts were already feeling the effects of the green paste: I myself had experienced a complete transformation of the sense of taste. The water that I drank seemed to have the savor of the most exquisite wine, meat turned to raspberries in my mouth, and raspberries to meat. I should not have been able to distinguish a chop from a peach.

Baudelaire visited the Club des Haschischins once, but condemned hashish for destroying free will, an interesting position for someone addicted to opium. "No man who, with a spoonful of jam, can gain instant access to all the delights of heaven and earth, will ever exert himself to acquire the thousandth part of them by dint of hard work." Hashish is meant for idle wastrels, he said, and under the influence of the poison, man becomes the ultimate living expression of the self-centeredness of passion. Yet Baudelaire left a recipe for hashish jam in the *Poem of Hashish,* noting that hashish resin may be taken with chocolate or ginger sweets:

> The oily extract of hashish as prepared by the Arabs is obtained by boiling the tops of the green plant in butter with a little water. When all the moisture has evaporated the mixture is strained, yielding a substance that looks like a greenish-yellow ointment and smells unpleasantly of hashish and rancid butter. In this form it is used in little pellets of two to four grams; but because of its repulsive odor, which increases with time, the Arabs disguise the extract in sweetmeats.
>
> The most commonly used of these confections, dawamesk, is a mixture of extract, sugar, and various flavorings, such as vanilla, cinnamon, pistachio, almond or musk. Sometimes even a little Spanish fly is added, but this is to achieve effects that have nothing in common with those usually created by hashish. In this form hashish is not at all disagreeable, and can be taken in doses of fifteen, twenty, or thirty grams, either in a wafer of unleavened bread or in a cup of coffee.

What is so important about this last message from Pomme? I still don't recall that Flaubert ever took hashish jam. I'm listlessly paging through Flaubert's published letters now, hoping to find a clue to what she meant, to my nausea. Why is my skin so rough, almost scaly? Why can I barely keep my hand on the page or focus my concentration?

Pomme used to criticize me for what she called my casual cruelty. She found me too much aligned with the men whose work I read and admire, and then she despised me and railed against the attraction she held for me despite her disgust. Now I think our affair is about to make its disastrous effect fully known in a way I could never have imagined.

Slow, tedious hours of sorting through my library, tracing everything having to do with Flaubert, and I've finally found the letter that inspired Pomme to this act of madness. I once gave Pomme a copy of Flaubert's collected letters when I thought she would appreciate them. She has used them against me. "The taste of arsenic was so real in my mouth when I described how Emma Bovary was poisoned, that it cost me two indigestions one upon the other—quite real ones, for I vomited my dinner."

I can barely move.

1. CONSOMMÉ À LA DESLIGNAC

Consommé à la Deslignac is a chicken consommé thickened with tapioca and garnished with diced Royale, stuffed and poached lettuce leaves, and shredded chervil.

Royale is moulded custard cut into shapes to garnish clear soups. Tapioca comes from the root of the manioc plant and is a thickener for soups and desserts.

RISSOLES OF YOUNG RABBIT WITH TRUFFLES

Rissoles are small deep fried pastries, like turnovers, with various sweet or savory fillings.

GNOQUIS OF POTATOES (ZOLA CALLS THEM *NIOKYS*)

From *The Household Cookery Book,* Félix Urbain-Dubois, 1871

Let boil, in water, eight or ten potatoes with their peel on; peel them, grate them, or pass them through a sieve; place this purée in a stewpan, season it, mix into it a piece of butter, one whole egg, two yolks of eggs, and a handful of grated parmesan; pour the preparation then on the floured slab, introduce into it, working with both hands, a third of its volume of flour; immediately divide the paste into several parts, which roll to strings of the thickness of a finger; cut these strings transversally, round the cut parts; let them poach in salted water; as soon they have got firm, drain them, put them into a flat stewpan, pour over them melted butter, sprinkle over grated parmesan cheese, pour on a little gravy, and dish them up.

CARP À LA CHAMBOURD

Chambourd is a classic and complicated method of preparing large whole fish. The fish is stuffed and braised in red wine and garnished with a mixture of quenelles of fish forcemeat, fillets of sole, sautéed roes, mushroom caps, truffles, and crayfish.

SADDLE OF VENISON À L'ANGLAISE

Venison cooked à l'Anglaise is boiled in a white stock.

PULLETS À LA MARÉCHALE

These are chicken breasts coated with egg and bread crumbs and sautéed. They are garnished with bundles of asparagus tips and a slice of truffle (a Maréchale garnish) and served with butter or thickened chateaubriand sauce. Chateaubriand sauce is a reduction of chopped shallots, thyme, bay leaf, mushroom parings, and white wine.

SALAD OF SOLE-FILLETS, WITH RAVIGOTE SAUCE
From *The Household Cookery Book*, Félix Urbain-Dubois, 1871

Plunge three cleansed soles into salted and acidulated water; at the first bubbling, remove the stewpan back to side; ten minutes after, drain the soles, let them nearly cool, then disengage the fillets of both sides, trim them regularly to equal length, place them on a dish, season them, pour over oil and vinegar.

Prepare a vegetable salad, season it, and thicken it with a little limed mayonnaise sauce. When firm, range it in a pyramid shape, on the centre of a cold dish: place the fillets of soles in an upright position, side by side, leaning them against the pyramid. Set on the top of it a bunch of chopped aspic jelly; surround the base with jelly "croutons"; serve separately a sauceboatful of ravigote-sauce.

RAVIGOTE SAUCE
Adapted from *The Escoffier Cookbook* (the American edition of
Guide Culinaire, 1903), Auguste Escoffier

Mix together 1 pint of olive oil, ⅓ pint of vinegar, salt and pepper to taste, 2 ounces capers, 3 tablespoons fine herbs. (The fine herbs are a blend of equal amounts of finely chopped onion and parsley, and a half amount each of chopped chervil, tarragon, and chives.) Stir vigorously.

CÈPES À L'ITALIENNE

Cèpes are a kind of mushroom. Sauce à l'Italienne is a mayonnaise sauce with lemon juice garnished with dice of brains and chopped parsley.

PINEAPPLE FRITTERS À LA FAVORITE
Adapted from *The Escoffier Cookbook* (the American edition of
Guide Culinaire, 1903), Auguste Escoffier

Prepare a frangipan cream, chill, and mix with chopped pistachios.

Cut a pineapple into ⅓ inch slices. Cut each slice in half and sprinkle with sugar and kirsch. Let sit for 30 minutes. Pat slices dry and dip into chilled frangipan cream.

Prepare a thin batter. Dip pineapple slices in batter and fry in plenty of hot fat. Drain and sprinkle with confectioner's sugar, glaze in a hot oven, and serve.

FRANGIPAN CREAM

Mix together ½ pound of confectioner's sugar, 2 ounces flour, 2 eggs, and 5 egg yolks. Pour 1 pint boiling milk over this mixture and stir briskly. Add a pinch of salt and any flavoring desired. Pour cream into a saucepan and stir over a medium flame. Let the mixture boil for a few minutes. Pour into a bowl and add 3 tablespoons butter and 2 tablespoons dry, crushed macaroons. Mix well. Smooth the surface of the cream with a buttered spoon to prevent a crust from forming while it cools.

2. BÉCHAMEL SAUCE
Adapted from *Larousse Gastronomique,* 1984

Béchamel sauce was named for one of Louis XIV's courtiers, Marquis de Béchamel, although according to *Larousse Gastronomique* another courtier claimed credit for serving the sauce decades before the Marquis de Béchamel was even born. The sauce is a white roux—a blend of flour and melted butter—flavored with a clove-studded onion.

Melt 3 tablespoons of butter over low heat. Add 6 tablespoons of flour and stir until well blended without allowing it to change color. Add 2 cups of milk and whisk to prevent lumps from forming. Season with salt, pepper, and grated nutmeg. Continue to cook the sauce slowly until it reaches the desired consistency, stirring it occasionally to prevent a skin from forming.

3. CHEESECAKE MADE FROM BRIE
From *Grand Dictionnaire de Cuisine,* Alexandre Dumas, 1873

Take some fine Brie cheese, knead it with a litre of flour, 90 grams of butter and a little salt. Add five or six eggs and thin the dough well, working it with the palm of your hand. Next, let it rest for half an hour; then roll it out with a rolling pin. Shape the cake in the usual way, brush it with egg, put in the oven to cook, and serve.

4 .   M U L L E D   W I N E
Adapted from *Larousse Gastronomique,* 1984

Heat a bottle of Léoville over a low flame with lemon or orange peel, sugar or honey, and spices (cinnamon, cloves, mace), but do not allow to boil. After about 10 minutes, strain the wine and serve. (The spices may also be soaked in a glass of the wine for 30 minutes before heating.)

P Ê C H E S   À   L A   C O N D É

Foods prepared à la Condé are named for the French general Condé the Great (1621–1686.) Pêches à la Condé are poached and served on rice that has been cooked in milk, sugar, and vanilla, and topped with fruit syrup.

5 .   M A C A R O O N S

According to *Larousse Gastronomique,* macaroons originated in Italy, possibly dating to 791 when they were made at the monastery at Cormery. During the seventeenth century in France, macaroons were prepared by Carmelite nuns who considered almonds good for girls who do not eat meat. (Colette, on the other hand, cautioned women not to eat too many almonds as they put weight on the breasts.) Classic macaroons are hard on the outside and soft inside.

Lightly whisk 4 egg whites with a pinch of salt.

Mix together 1½ cups of sugar and 3 cups of ground almonds, and whisk with egg whites.

Spoon small heaps of the mixture, spacing them well apart, onto a baking tray that has been lined with greased wax paper. Bake at 400°F for about 12 minutes. Transfer to a wire rack to cool.

6 . PUNCH

Named after the Hindustani word for five, punch is an iced or hot drink made from five principal ingredients: water, sugar, aromatic spices, fruit, and alcohol. On April 9, 1814, Byron wrote to Thomas Moore and described the Regency punch that he had enjoyed with his lobster.

THE REGENT'S PUNCH
From *Modern Cookery,* Eliza Acton, 1850

Pare as thin as possible the rinds of two China oranges, of two lemons, and of one Seville orange, and infuse them for an hour in half a pint of thick cold syrup; then add to them the juice of the fruit. Make a pint of strong green tea, sweeten it well with fine sugar, and when it is quite cold, add it to the fruit and syrup, with a glass of the best old Jamaica rum, a glass of brandy, one of arrack, one of pine-apple syrup, and two bottles of champagne; pass the whole thing through a fine lawn sieve until it is perfectly clear, then bottle, and put it into ice until dinner is served. We are indebted for this receipt to a person who made the punch daily for the prince's table, at Carlton palace, for six months; it has been in our possession for some years, and may be relied on.

Rinds and juice of 2 China oranges, 2 lemons, and of 1 Seville orange; syrup, ½ pint; strong green tea, sweetened, 1 pint; best old Jamaica rum, arrack, French brandy (vieux cognac), and pine-apple syrup, each 1 glassful; champagne, 2 bottles. In ice for a couple of hours.

Arrack, one of the ingredients called for in this recipe, was a liquor from the East Indies made from rice, sugar, and dates and flavored with spices and fruit juices.

7 . RICE CAKES
Adapted from *Beeton's Book of Household Management,* Isabella Beeton, 1859–1861

Isabella Beeton gives a recipe for rice cakes that requires ¼ pound of sugar, ¼ pound of butter, and 2 eggs for every ½ pound of rice flour. The butter is beaten, flour and sugar are added, and finally the eggs. Roll out the dough, cut into rounds, and bake for 12 to 18 minutes in a slow oven.

8. SALAD APHRODITE
From *The Alice B. Toklas Cookbook,* Alice B. Toklas, 1954

Recommended for poets with delicate digestions. Mix finely chopped apples and celery with yoghurt, salt, and pepper and serve on a bed of crisp lettuce.

CHAPTER NINE

Gifts from a
Literary Kitchen

POMME'S HOUSEHOLD BOOK

M F. K. Fisher said that when she wrote about food, she was really writing about love. So a gift of food is simply a gift of love, the supreme expression of this being a remarkable Thai custom requiring a dying person to prepare a collection of recipes for the mourners. When I think or write about food and when I prepare food, I am thinking about life, its textured layers constantly shifting, its abundant small transformations leading to epiphanies, its artistry and mystery enhanced by the senses and by love. With one exception, the gifts from my kitchen have always been gifts of life.

I'll begin to gather my recipes now, an eventual keepsake for all my friends, but for the moment my private household book, a work in progress. In Willa Cather's home, handwritten recipes and notes were slipped inside cookbooks, transforming published works into household books. Women who owned no cookbooks exchanged recipes for foods, cosmetics, and cures with neighbors and friends. Their homemade household books served as journals, commemorated their friendships and communities, and told their stories.

Martha Lloyd, who lived with Jane Austen's family, compiled recipes for brewing fruit wines, curing meat, baking cheesecakes, whitening stockings, and making potpourris and ink—the last being the most important recipe in the Austen household. The ink was made by steeping gauls (an acid made from oak apples) and green copperas (iron sulfate) in beer and sugar for two weeks. Now my pen is freshly filled and I shall begin.

Gifts of Love

Twin loaves of bread have just been born into the world under my auspices—fine children, the image of their mother.

—Emily Dickinson

If you are a cook and your friend loves literature, wrap together a box of marzipan and a copy of *La Rabouilleuse* by Balzac in which the sweet is described. Give Emily Dickinson's black cake along with a book of her poems. Emily dispatched currant wines, breads, and candy accompanied by poetry or slips of paper bearing fond sayings. "I enclose Love's 'remainder bisquit' somewhat scorched perhaps in the baking but Love's oven is warm!" read a note that Emily enclosed with a batch of caramels for her sister-in-law. Or bake Jane Carlyle's bread, a fine crusty loaf, and present it with a copy of the cookbook she used.

After a single life spent cultivating her mind, the newly married Jane Carlyle was thrust unprepared into domesticity. When her husband, Thomas Carlyle, suffered stomach trouble from eating bread bought in town, Jane taught herself how to bake. Using William Cobbett's *Cottage Economy,* she started her dough too late in the day, put the bread in the oven at bedtime, and was obliged to stay up well into the night to finish the project. She wrote to a friend that as she waited for the bread to bake, she felt like the artist

Benvenuto Cellini with his cast of Perseus in the oven. Did Thomas respond to Jane's efforts, as William Cobbett suggested he might?

> Give me, for a beautiful sight, a neat and smart woman, heating her oven and setting in her bread! And, if the bustle do make the sign of labour glisten on her brow, where is the man that would not kiss that off, rather than lick the plaster from the cheek of a duchess?

Bread baking has somehow taken on a mysterious quality, making it seem an intimidating act for many people. The secret to making good bread is that there is no secret. Let your imagination help you break any rules you imagine exist to daunt you. Don't let cookbook writers like Cobbett, who took four pages to tell his readers how to make bread, scare you from the kitchen. Although once you recover from his attitude, his recipes are good ones. The bread recipe I use is simple and the possibility for variations are endless.

POMME'S BREAD

2¾ cups white flour
½ cup whole-wheat flour
1 packet (¼ ounce) of dry yeast
½ teaspoon salt
1½ cups water or milk or a mixture of both
2 tablespoons butter or lard
2 tablespoons sugar

Heat 1 cup of milk until it is very warm to the touch. Add sugar and yeast. Let stand for a few minutes.

Put the flour into a large mixing bowl, add the salt, and make a well in the center. Add the fat, and then add the milk and yeast, and blend. Knead until you have a soft, pliable dough, adding more flour or liquid as necessary.

Cover and let rise in a greased bowl in a warm place for an hour or until double in bulk. Punch down and knead again. Shape into a loaf or divide into rolls and let rise on the baking sheet until doubled again. Preheat oven to 350°F and bake for 45 minutes to one hour.

Variations

The butter yields a soft, uniform crumb, but it is not an essential ingredient. For different flavor, add grated nutmeg to the flour, or saffron, or garlic powder, or anything else you feel like.

Bread is a homey gift of the hearth. A cake is a luxury, a more extravagant gift. Emily Dickinson reciprocated a present of bulbs with a slice of rich black cake, a copy of her recipe, and flowers from the bulbs.

BLACK CAKE

From *Emily Dickinson: Profile of the Poet as Cook,* Guides at the Dickinson Homestead, 1976

2 lbs. flour
2 lbs. sugar
2 lbs. butter
19 eggs
5 lbs. raisins
1¼ lbs. currants
1¼ lbs. citron
½ pint brandy

½ pint molasses

2 teaspoons nutmeg

5 teaspoons cloves, mace, and cinnamon

2 teaspoons soda

Blend sugar and butter. Add eggs. Blend dry ingredients and mix all together.

Bake at 250°F for 5–6 hours.

Black cakes, like wedding and Christmas cakes, might be topped by marzipan. Balzac described marzipan or Massepains d'Issoudun in *La Rabouilleuse* as a rich and guarded secret of the ancient religious order of Ursuline nuns. Four years after the book's publication in 1840, a rumor had Balzac opening a pâtissière in the rue Vivienne in Paris where he planned to sell the Massepains d'Issoudun. Whether Balzac involved himself with such a venture is unknown, but the talk reflamed public interest in his novel.

MARZIPAN
Adapted from *Larousse Gastronomique,* 1984

Grind 3½ cups of blanched almonds with 2 cups of sugar and ¼ cup of vanilla sugar. Gradually add 4 egg whites. Let the mixture rest for a few minutes. Roll the paste to a thickness of ¼ inch and cut into shapes with a cookie cutter. Frost the pieces with slightly liquid royal icing flavored with a few drops of orangeflower water. Lay the marzipan on a baking sheet lined with waxed paper, and dry out in a cool oven.

ROYAL ICING

Gradually add some confectioner's sugar to lightly beaten egg whites, stirring continuously until it forms a mixture thick enough to spread without running. Stop stirring when the mixture is smooth. A few drops of flavoring may be added (10 drops for every 2 egg whites). To frost cakes, use 1 egg white per 1⅓ cups of sugar.

I had a lover who delighted in the gifts from my kitchen until he traveled to Singapore and disappeared. I heard from him a few months later. He had been arrested for drug smuggling. He recently wrote to me to ask for more notebooks and said he's making good progress on his novel. If I could also send him gifts of food to comfort him, then I would. At least he has learned how to use his solitude.

How to Nurture Artistry and Passion

This Bouillabaisse a noble dish is—
A sort of soup, or broth, or brew,
Or hotchpotch of all sorts of fishes,
That Greenwich never could outdo:
Green herbs, red peppers, mussels, saffron,
Soles, onions, garlic, roach, and dace:
All these you eat at Terré's tavern
In that one dish of Bouillabaisse.
—William Makepeace Thackeray
from *The Ballad of Bouillabaisse*

The culinary talent I wish for my friends, my lovers, my favorite students, is the ability to prepare a perfect bouillabaisse, the rich fish soup from the south of France that exemplifies the pursuit of perfection. *Larousse Gastronomique* describes how fishermen made the soup in cauldrons on the beach, using fish considered unsuitable for market, but the origins of the dish remain murky and hotly disputed. Those who take the task of making bouillabaisse seriously believe that of the hundreds of ways to prepare bouil-labaisse, theirs is the right way.

Some argue that the fish must be cooked whole in the pot, removed from the broth at the last moment of cooking, and served separately. Some cut the fish into pieces, others serve the fish in the soup. Alice B. Toklas pronounced that a bouillabaisse should in-clude at least five varieties of fish and that three kinds of bouillabaisse exist in France: the authentic one of Marseilles, which calls for Mediterranean fish; a Parisian version made from fish born in the Atlantic Ocean; and "a very false one indeed made of fresh-water fish." Ford Madox Ford, bitterly disappointed in the oil-based cooking of Provence, regarded bouillabaisse as the bright spot in the cuisine of the South. In his mind, the three schools of bouillabaisse cookery were distinguished not by the origins of the fish but by whether the soup contained langouste or potatoes or neither. "I favour potatoes and no langouste," he wrote in *Provence*. Waverly Root believed that every town in France produces its own version of bouillabaisse, but all share three essential ingredients— olive oil, tomatoes, and saffron.

BOUILLABAISSE
Ford's Adaptation of Chef Caillat's recipe, Marseilles, 1891,
from *Provence,* Ford Madox Ford

Take then large quantities of the fish called *rascasse*—for which my dictionary gives no translation; of the *grondin*—the red gurnet of the

North Sea; of the *boudroie,* for which again I have no translation; of the conger eel; of the *roucaou;* of the *merlan,* or whiting; of the *Saint Pierre,* otherwise the *zée* which my dictionary calls the *zeus-fish,* which Larousse states to be a genus of Australian (!) though you see it caught every day in the Mediterranean, I believe it to be a species of haddock. And last of all you take the *loup du rocher,* the most radiant, the most delicate and the most costly of all the fishes of all the seas and rivers that God has made, its flesh having the firmness of the finest trout, a consistency and whiteness of its own and a complete absence of the slight suspicion of aftertaste of mud that mars the finest of Scottish brook trout.

Having chosen very fresh specimens of these fish, scale and clean them and cut them in vertical slices; set aside the whiting, the *loup,* the *zée* and the *roucaou,* which being more delicate calls for less cooking.

Place in a saucepan a minced onion, two tomatoes and three or four cloves of garlic, some fennel, bay, and peel of bitter orange all equally minced fine, a sprig of thyme; add the fish that you did not set aside, a quarter of a pint of olive oil, pepper, salt and saffron; just cover with boiling water and place on a quick fire so that it may come quickly to the boil. Five minutes later add the remaining fish; keep boiling five minutes longer, always very quickly so that the mixing may be thorough.

Have ready on a soup plate or tureen slices of bread one-third of an inch in thickness; pour the bouillon over this whilst straining it; arrange the fish on another dish, removing the pot-herbs, sprinkle with parsley and serve.

Room exists in the world for all sorts of bouillabaisse. Serious cooks must not close their minds to other ways of seeing and sensing and tasting. Acknowledge the artistry of another cook. You may become better for your willingness to learn.

I often wondered what my father considers his greatest achievement in the kitchen. I've learned much from him about boldness and about nurturing my passion, but I wondered what lay at the source of his own spirited culinary imagination. I asked him to send me the recipe he considers symbolic of his artistry in the kitchen. His response:

Chérie,

I have been thinking carefully about the recipe you asked for.

Should I give you the one for pasta that I borrowed from our old friend Étienne that earned me my last promotion? (Did you hear that a few years ago, after he left his position at Chez Robert, he joined the Foreign Legion? We've not heard from him since.)

Or should I recall for you the heart-shaped, hand-dipped chocolates filled with frangipani cream that I created for your mother when we first met? Or perhaps I could tell you about the dishes I served at Chez Robert when the Savoy Hotel managers came to scout for new chefs. All these have been significant recipes in my life.

I decided instead to create a new recipe for you. The past is gone and so an old recipe cannot represent me in my constant exploration for new and intriguing flavors to please me and my guests. The recipe, because it is a gift, underscores the fact that artists need to share their creations, particularly with the ones they love. Last, the recipe is simple but its potential for variation is wide, and the splash of brandy or calvados gives the dish an unexpected bite. I like to surprise.

FEU D'ENFER FOR POMME

Wash and hull strawberries or raspberries. If the strawberries are large, slice them in half.

Cut a banana into chunks.

Heat a tablespoon or so of butter with two tablespoons of sugar in a frying pan over a medium flame. When the mixture starts to bubble, add the banana slices and sauté for a few minutes, stirring the fruit as it cooks. Add the berries and sauté for several more minutes.

Add a jigger of brandy or calvados or another spirit and set the liquor alight in the pan. Serve immediately over ice cream.

I am anxious to know what you think of this dish. I thought it would go well with the Biscuits Tortoni I know you enjoy. The heat of the fruit and the chill of the ice cream perform a kind of alchemy to yield an extravagant flavor in your mouth.

Your loving father,
Henri

When I seek inspiration in the kitchen, I dine on foods that complement my hungry mind's search. I love the fiery dessert that my father created for me, but I save that for particularly restless occasions. Sometimes I fortify my creative progress with the cold flip that Charles Dickens drank during intermissions of his public readings, a recipe that he mentions in *Little Dorrit*—"The yolk of a new-laid egg, beaten up with a glass of sound sherry, nutmeg and powdered sugar." Other times I warm myself with the cocoa suggested by François Tassart, valet to Guy de Maupassant. While Maupassant studied in the kitchen, Tassart served him hot chocolate flavored with a vanilla pod warmed over the stove for twelve hours. I simply add half a teaspoon of vanilla to my cup of cocoa.

Maupassant and Tassart once traveled together on a weekend visit to a house where Flaubert was also staying. A butler loaned a copy of *Madame Bovary* to Tassart, who read the novel aloud in installments to the other servants, prompting lively discussions about Emma Bovary. One of the maids declared that if she were Emma, she would have feigned affection for the poacher, then seized his gun and killed him to protect her secret.

Read *Madame Bovary,* think about what you would have done if you were Emma, then sip from Flaubert's hot toddy. Alice B. Toklas gives his recipe in her cookbook. Warm two jiggers of calvados and one jigger of apricot brandy, and slowly and carefully pour one jigger of cream into the spirits. Or drink Evelyn Waugh's restorative, prepared for him after a night out with "some charming Norwegians" in Athens in 1929.

PEPPERED CHAMPAGNE
From *When the Going Was Good,* Evelyn Waugh, 1929

He took a large tablet of beet sugar (an equivalent quantity of ordinary lump sugar does equally well) and soaked it in Angostura Bitters and then rolled it in Cayenne pepper. This he put into a large glass which he filled up with champagne. The excellences of this drink defy description. The sugar and Angostura enrich the wine and take away that slight acidity which renders even the best champagne repugnant in the early morning. Each bubble as it rises to the surface carries with it a red grain of pepper, so that as one drinks one's appetite is at once stimulated and gratified, heat and cold, fire and liquid, contending on one's palate and alternating in the mastery of one's sensations. I sipped this almost unendurably desirable drink.

I once sipped an unendurably desirable drink, utterly seduced by its poison. If you've ever contemplated revenge, beware of where your thoughts might lead. Colette retaliated against her second husband by conducting an affair with his adolescent son, her stepson. Had she taken time to reconsider her malicious act, would she have used the young man in that way? Understand how passion makes you strong, but know also when it renders you weak, when it blinds you. What act of wickedness would you inflict on someone merely because you did not get your way? Before you embrace vengeance, remove yourself from your selfish interior life. Go outside and walk and observe and learn from the world. There is artistry and solace in everything and everyone. Let them feed you. Learn to harness your passions, your appetites. After your invigorating walk in the world, when you have properly considered your motives, if you still desire revenge, well, at least your vengeance will be a true act, rather than a blindly passionate one.

Consider Emily Dickinson's thoughts on the matter:

> Mine Enemy is growing old—
> I have at last Revenge—
> The Palate of the Hate departs—
> If any would avenge
>
> Let him be quick—the Viand flits—
> It is a faded Meat—
> Anger as soon as fed is dead—
> 'Tis starving makes it fat—

But I fed my own anger too quickly. Had I thought more carefully about the mortal dangers lurking in my pretty jars of redcurrant jam, then I might have refrained from such rash behavior. But then, as Emily said, denying my anger might have fattened it. Could my revenge have assumed an even more sinister form?

If you are very angry and your walk is a long one, you will need nourishment on your expedition, in which case you should pack a picnic lunch.

Recipes for a Thoughtful Excursion

The guiding rule for picnic baskets might be taken from Henry James, who said they should be "not so good as to fail of an amusing disorder, nor yet so bad as to defeat the proper function of repast." Evelyn Waugh once described a picnic of tea and banana sandwiches. The key to making a successful banana sandwich is slicing the bananas finely and arranging them on buttered homemade bread. The exactness required to prevent the bananas from squelching out after the first bite would have appealed to Henry James's sense of precision.

Charles Dickens and Wilkie Collins traveled through Europe in the mid-1800s, heading for Chamonix, as Dickens wrote in a letter home, "with a Strasbourg sausage, a bottle of wine, brandy, kirsch-wasser and plenty of bread to keep off hunger on the road." They reached Bolsena, an Italian lake town near Orvieto, where once a year the citizens blanket the streets in flowers, and Dickens reported that they "made a great fire, and strengthened the country wine with some brandy (we always carry brandy) and mulled it with cloves (we always carry cloves) and went to bed." Since reading Dickens's letters, I carry cloves as well as cardamom in my pockets. Their pungent flavors sweeten the breath.

TO MULL WINE
(An excellent French recipe)
From *Modern Cookery,* Eliza Acton, 1850

Boil in a wineglassful and a half of water, a quarter of an ounce of spice (cinnamon, ginger slightly bruised, and cloves), with three ounces of fine sugar, until they form a thick syrup, which must not on any account be allowed to burn. Pour in a pint of port wine, and stir it gently until it is on the point of boiling only: it should then be served immediately. The addition of a strip or two of orange-rind cut extremely thin, gives to this beverage the flavour of bishop. In France, light claret takes the place of port wine in making it, and the better kinds of vin du pays are very palatable thus prepared.

Sherry, or very fine raisin, or ginger wine, prepared as above, and stirred hot to the yolks of four fresh eggs, will be found excellent.

You are lucky if you've taken long rambling walks in the countryside to pick the blackberries growing wild. Read *Cider With Rosie,* by Laurie Lee, to immerse yourself in fresh wheaty smells and open vistas of English landscapes. If there are any berries left after your outing, if you tire of cramming them into your mouth, then there are wonderful things to do with them just as soon as you've wiped the purple stains from your chin.

O, blackberry tart, with berries as big as your thumb, purple and black, and thick with juice, and a crust to endear them that will go to cream in your mouth, and both passing down with such a taste that will make you close your eyes and wish you might live forever in the wideness of that rich moment.
—Richard Llewellyn
How Green Was My Valley

Your excursion should soothe your angry thoughts. Think about the one you love. If he or she meets your devoted attention with cool indifference, how will you feel and what will you do? I acted impetuously, selfishly. Now I would try to understand the nature of the lesson to be learned about myself, about love, and then I would move on. Perhaps I should have made a generous blackberry pie for Jeremy, and then simply forgiven him.

JEREMY'S BLACKBERRY PIE
Pâte Sucrée or Piecrust

Combine 2 cups sifted all-purpose flour, 4 tablespoons of sugar, ¼ teaspoon salt. Work in ¾ cup of softened butter.

Make a well in the dough and add 2 egg yolks, 1 teaspoon vanilla, 2 tablespoons water. Blend until the dough forms a ball. Cover and chill for at least 30 minutes.

Roll to ⅛ thickness for piecrust, and line greased pie pan with pastry.

Blackberry Filling

Combine ⅔ to 1 cup sugar, ¼ cup flour. (If the fruit is wet, add 2 teaspoons cornstarch to the dry ingredients.) Sprinkle dry ingredients over 4 cups of fresh berries, and toss lightly until fruit is coated. Let stand for 15 minutes.

Preheat oven to 450°F.

Turn the fruit into the pie shell and dot with 1–2 tablespoons butter. Cover the fruit with a piecrust lattice or a well-pricked pastry top. Bake for 10 minutes. Reduce heat to 350°F and bake 35–40 minutes or until golden brown.

If you are in a regretful mood, despondent and sad, comfort yourself with pleasant visions of an early morning meal on a Parisian terrace, overlooking a cobblestoned courtyard, or with thoughts of rough and hearty country foods served in a rustic country inn, of Katherine Mansfield's sunlit experience of breakfast on the Continent in 1920:

> It grew hot. Everywhere the light quivered green-gold. The white soft road unrolled, with plane-trees casting a trembling shade. There were piles of pumpkins and gourds: outside the house the tomatoes were spread in the sun. Blue flowers and red flowers and tufts of deep purple flared in the road-side hedges. A young boy, carrying a branch, stumbled across a yellow field, followed by a brown high-stepping little goat. We bought figs for breakfast, immense thin-skinned ones. They broke in one's fingers and tasted of wine and honey. Why is the northern fig such a chaste fair-haired virgin, such a soprano? The melting contraltos sing through the ages.

Or take instead the breakfast offered by Colette, soft-boiled eggs with cherries. "Try it: it's exquisite," wrote her friend Renée Hamon. Or the simple meal of eggs and bread and butter served to Henry James at an inn in Bourg-en-Bresse. "The eggs were so good that I am ashamed to say how many of them I consumed," he wrote in 1900 in *A Little Tour in France,* "and as for the butter nous sommes en Bresse et le beurre n'est pas mauvais, the landlady said with a sort of dry coquetry, as she placed this article before me. It was the poetry of butter, and I ate a pound of two of it; after which I came away with a strange mixture of impressions of late gothic sculpture and thick tartines." A tartine is a slice of bread generously spread with the poetry of butter or jam or pâté. An elaborate tartine might be spread with béchamel sauce, covered in grated cheese, and then deep-fried.

As you nurture yourself, finding patience and solace in your own company, try a slice of cake. A poem, written in 1881, appears in Emily Dickinson's handwriting on the reverse side of "Mrs. Carmichael's recipe for coconut cake."

The things that never can come back, are several—
Childhood—some forms of Hope—the Dead—
Though Joys—like Men—may sometimes make a Journey—
And still abide—
We do not mourn for Traveler, or Sailor,
Their Routes are fair—
But think enlarged of all that they will tell us
Returning here—
"Here!" There are typic "Heres"—
Foretold Locations—
The Spirit does not stand—
Himself—at whatsoever Fathom
His native Land—

COCONUT CAKE

From *Emily Dickinson: Profile of the Poet as Cook,* Guides at the
Dickinson Homestead, 1976

2 cups sugar
1 cups butter
2 cups flour
6 eggs
1 grated coconut
1 cup coconut milk

Cream butter and sugar. Gradually add flour, then beaten yolks. Beat whites separately, and fold in along with some grated coconut and coconut milk. Retain some coconut for coating the cake after baking and cake has been glazed with simple sugar icing. Fill cake pans half full and bake at 350°F for 25–30 minutes. This is a very rich, heavy cake.

If your regrets linger, if you cannot find inspiration in solitude, then you still have much to learn from the writers and the poets and the cooks on becoming the artist of your own life. The things that never can come back are several, and you can never re-create the past. But you can shape your own future. And you can make a cake.

Eat the cake slowly and consider how you might perfect the art of living. "With her the art of living came before the art of writing," wrote Maurice Goudeket about Colette, praising her for her country wisdom, her range of household accomplishments from making orange wine to cooking truffles to preserving linen. "Looked at in one light," he said, "it would not have displeased her if one talked of recipes for writing." In the summertime, Colette gathered berries and placed them into a cask where the brandy imbibed a tart and fruity flavor.

Now pour a generous glass of Colette's fruited marc brandy and raise it for my final toast, a recipe for an epigram by William Somerset Maugham from *A Writer's Notebook:*

The Recipe: The young are earnest. He was a young man with a pugnacious but rather attractive face and a shock of thick brown hair. His inclinations were vaguely literary and he asked me how to make an epigram. Since he was in the flying corps it seemed natural enough to answer: 'You merely loop the loop on a commonplace and come down between the lines.' His brow puckered as he turned my reply over in his mind. He was paying me the compliment of giving it his serious attention: I only wanted the tribute of a smile.

All I want is the tribute of a smile.

Classics in the Kitchen: An Edible Anthology for the Literary Gourmet, by Jean Aaberg and Judith Homme Bulduc. Los Angeles: Ward Ritchie Press, 1969.

A Treatise on Adulterations of Food and Culinary Poisons, by Frederick Accum. Philadelphia: Ab'm Small, 1820.

The Best of Eliza Action: Recipes from her Classic Modern Cookery for Private Families, selected and edited by Elizabeth Ray with an introduction by Elizabeth David. London: Longman, 1968.

Modern Cookery for Private Families, by Eliza Acton. London: Longman, Green & Co., 1850, 1887.

Poems by Eliza Acton. Ipswich: R. Deck, 1826.

Monsieur Proust, by Céleste Albaret, edited by Georges Belmont. New York: McGraw-Hill, 1976.

A History of Private Life, v. III, Passions of the Renaissance, Philippe Ariès and Georges Duby, general editors, edited by Roger Chartier. Cambridge: Belknap Press of Harvard University Press, 1989.

L'Académie Goncourt en Dix Couverts, edited by Eduoard Aubarel. George Ravon, 1943.

Journey to a War, by W. H. Auden and Christopher Isherwood. London: Faber & Faber, 1939.

Jane Austen's Letters to Her Sister Cassandra and Others, collected and edited by R. W. Chapman. Oxford: Clarendon Press, 1932.

The Letters of Jane Austen, selected by Sarah Chauncey Woolsey. Boston: Little, Brown, 1903.

The Cookery of the British Isles, by Adrian Bailey and the editors of Time-Life Books. New York: Time-Life, 1969.

Dinner at Magny's, by Robert Baldick. London: Victor Gollancz, 1971.

La Rabouilleuse, by Honoré de Balzac. Translated by George Ives. Philadelphia: G. Barrie & Son, 1897. First published in 1840.

The Letters of Honoré de Balzac to Madame Hanska from *The Works of Balzac,* by Honoré de Balzac. Boston: Little, Brown, 1899–1900.

Splendors and Miseries of Courtesans, by Honoré de Balzac. Philadelphia: George Barrie & Son, 1895.

Gluttons and Libertines: Human Problems of Being Natural, by Marston Bates. New York: Random House, 1967. First published in 1958.

Intimate Journals, by Charles Baudelaire, translated by Christopher Isherwood, introduction by W. H. Auden. Hollywood: Marcel Rodd, 1947.

Poem of Hashish, by Charles Baudelaire, and *The Haschish Club,* by Théophile Gautier, translated by John Githers. New York: Harper & Row, 1971.

Beard on Bread, by James Beard. New York: Alfred A. Knopf, 1973.

Delights and Prejudices, by James Beard. New York: Atheneum, 1964.

America Day by Day, by Simone de Beauvoir. New York: Grove Press, 1953.

And Even Now, by Max Beerbohm. London: William Heinemann, 1920, 1921.

Beeton's Book of Household Management, by Mrs. Isabella Beeton. Facsimile of first edition, 1861. London: Chancellor Press, 1991.

Mrs. Beeton's All About Cookery, by Isabella Beeton. London: Ward Lock & Co., 1961.

Mrs. Beeton's Family Cookery, by Isabella Beeton. London: Ward Lock & Co., 1923.

Paris Cafes: Their Role in the Birth of Modern Art, by Georges Bernier. New York: Wildenstein, 1985.

The Last of the Bohemians: Twenty Years with Leon-Paul Fargue, by André Beucler, introduction by Archibald MacLeish. Westport: Greenwood Press, 1954.

Love, by Marie Henrie Beyle. London: Merlin Press, 1957. First published in 1822.

Memoirs of an Egotist, by Marie Henri Beyle. London: Turnstile Press, 1949. First published in 1892.

The Private Diaries of Stendhal (Marie Henri Beyle), edited and translated by Robert Sage. New York: Doubleday, 1954.

Emily Dickinson Face to Face: Unpublished Letters with Notes and Reminiscences, by Martha Dickinson Bianchi. Boston: Houghton Mifflin, 1932.

Vie des Frères Goncourt, 3 v., by Andre Billy. Les Editions de l'imprimerie nationale de Monaco, 1956.

Boswell's London Journal, by James Boswell, introduction and notes by Frederick Pottle. New York: Macmillan, 1950.

The Life of Samuel Johnson, by James Boswell. New York: Viking Penguin, 1987. First published in 1791.

Les Restaurants dans la Comédie Humaine, by Patrice Boussel. Paris: Editions de la Tournelle, 1950.

British Gastronomy: The Rise of Great Restaurants, by Gregory Houston Bowden. London: Chatto and Windus, 1975.

Café Society: Bohemian Life from Swift to Bob Dylan, by Steve Bradshaw. London: Weidenfeld & Nicholson, 1978.

The New Art of Cookery According to the Present Practice; Being a Complete Guide to all Housekeepers, by Richard Briggs. Philadelphia, 1792.

The Physiology of Taste or Meditations on Transcendental Gastronomy, by Jean-Anthelme Brillat-Savarin. New Haven: Leete's Island Books, 1825.

Jane Eyre, by Charlotte Brontë. New York: Random House, 1943. First published in 1847.

Emily Dickinson: Profile of the Poet as Cook, by Guides at the Dickinson Homestead: Nancy Harris Brose, Juliana McGovern Dupre, Wendy Tocher Kohler, Jean McClure Mudge. Amherst, 1976.

Dinner Is Served, by Thomas Burke. London: George Routledge & Sons, 1937.

Don Juan, by Lord George Byron, edited and with an introduction by Leslie A. Marchand. Boston: Houghton Mifflin, 1958. First published in 1819–1824.

I Too Am Here: Selections from the Letters of Jane Welsh Carlyle. New York: Cambridge University Press, 1977.

History of My Life, by Giacomo Girolamo Casanova de Seigalt. New York: Harcourt Brace & World, 1966–1970. First published in 1826–1838.

The Foods and Wine of Spain, by Penelope Casas. New York: Alfred A. Knopf, 1991.

Willa Cather in Europe, by Willa Cather. New York: Alfred A. Knopf, 1956.

Love Letters of Great Men and Women, edited by C. A. Charles. London: Stanley Paul & Co., 1924.

This Must Be the Place: Memoirs of Montparnasse, by Jimmie the Barman (James Charters). London: Herbert Joseph Ltd., 1934.

"Thoughts for Food, I: French Cuisine and French Culture," by Priscilla Clark. *The French Review,* v. XLIX, no. 1, October 1975.

A Tramp Abroad, by Samuel Clemens. New York and London: Harper & Brothers, 1879, 1899, 1907.

Roughing It, by Samuel Clemens. Hartford: American Publishing Company, 1875.

The Innocents Abroad, by Samuel Clemens. Hartford: American Publishing Company, 1871.

What Shall We Have for Dinner, by Lady Maria Clutterbuck (Mrs. Charles Dickens). London: Bradbury & Evans, 1851.

Cottage Economy, by William Cobbett. London: Charles Griffin & Company, 1822, and 18th edition, 1867.

Professional Secrets: An Autobiography of Jean Cocteau Drawn from His Life of Writings, by Robert Phelps, translated by Richard Howard. New York: Farrar, Straus & Giroux, 1970.

Lui, a view of him, by Louise Colet. Athens: University of Georgia Press, 1986. First published in 1851.

The Blue Lantern, by Colette, translated by Roger Senhouse. New York: Farrar, Straus & Giroux, 1963. First published in 1949.

The Break of Day, by Colette, translated by Enid McLeod. London: Secker & Warburg, 1961. First published in 1928.

Chéri and the *Last of Chéri,* by Colette, translated by Roger Senhouse. New York: Farrar, Straus & Young, 1958. First published in 1920 and 1926.

Claudine Married from *The Complete Claudine,* by Colette, translated by An tonia White. New York: Farrar, Straus & Giroux, 1976. First published in 1902.

Claudine in Paris from *The Complete Claudine,* by Colette, translated by Antonia White. New York: Farrar, Straus & Giroux, 1976. First published in 1901.

Earthly Paradise: An Autobiography Drawn from Her Lifetime of Writings, by Robert Phelps. New York: Farrar, Straus & Giroux, 1966.

Mitsou or How Girls Grow Wise, by Colette. New York: Albert & Charles Boni, 1930.

My Apprenticeships, by Colette. London: Secker & Warburg, 1957. First published in 1936.

The Pure and the Impure, by Colette, translated by Herma Briffault. New York: Farrar, Straus & Giroux, 1966. First published in 1932 as *Ces Plaisirs.*

The Ripening Seed, by Colette, translated by Roger Senhouse. London: Secker & Warburg, 1955. First published in 1923.

The Tender Shoot, by Colette, translated by Antonia White. New York: Farrar, Straus, 1958.

La Treille Muscate de Colette. Eaux-fortes par André de Segonzac. 51 of 150 in print. Paris, 1932.

The Moonstone, by Wilkie Collins, edited by J. I. M. Stewart. London: Penguin, 1981. First published in 1868.

A Handbook of Cookery for a Small House, by Jessie Conrad, introduction by Joseph Conrad. New York: Doubleday, Page & Co., 1923.

Home Cookery, by Jessie Conrad, introduction by Joseph Conrad. London: Jarrolds Publishers, 1936.

Joseph Conrad: Times Remembered, by John Conrad. London and New York: Cambridge University Press, 1981.

The Savoy Was My Oyster, by Paolo Contarini. London: Robert Hale, 1976.

The English Table in History and Literature, by Charles Cooper. London: Sampson Low, Marston & Co., 1930.

Gleanings in Europe by an American, by James Fenimore Cooper. Philadelphia: Carey, Lea & Blanchard, 1837.

Colette, by Robert Cottrell. New York: Frederick Ungar Publishing, 1974.

Balzac à Table, by Courtine. Paris: Robert Laffont, 1976.

A Second Flowering: Work and Days of the Lost Generation, by Malcolm Cowley. New York: Viking Press, 1956.

Elizabeth David Classics: Mediterranean Food, French Country Cooking, Summer Cooking, by Elizabeth David. New York: Alfred A. Knopf, 1985.

English Bread and Yeast Cookery, by Elizabeth David. New York: Viking Press, 1980.

Italian Food, by Elizabeth David. New York: Alfred A. Knopf, 1958.

An Omelette and a Glass of Wine, by Elizabeth David. New York: Viking, 1985.

Summer Cooking, by Elizabeth David. London: Museum Press, 1955, 1961.

A Kipper with My Tea, by Allan Davidson. London: Macmillan, 1988.

Cafe Royal: Ninety Years of Bohemia, by G. Deghy and K. Waterhouse. London: Hutchinson 1955, 1956.

Confessions of an English Opium Eater, by Thomas de Quincey. London: Taylor & Hessey, 1822.

The Colour of Paris, by Messieurs les académiciens Goncourt, under the general editorship of M. Lucien Descaves. London: Chatto & Windus, 1908.

A Christmas Carol, by Charles Dickens. London: Macmillan, 1973. First published in 1843.

Little Dorrit, by Charles Dickens. Boston: P. Mason & Co., 1884. First published in 1855–1857.

The Cook and Housewife's Manual, by Meg Dods. 1819.

The Best Times, by John Dos Passos. New York: New American Library, 1966.

"Deciphering a Meal," by Mary Douglas. *Daedalus,* Journal of the American Academy of Arts and Sciences, Winter 1972: Myth, Symbol and Culture.

Venus in the Kitchen, by Pilaf Bey (pseud. for Norman Douglas). London: William Heinemann, 1952.

The Oxford Companion to English Literature, edited by Margaret Drabble. Oxford: Oxford University Press, 1985.

Pepys at Table, by Christopher Driver and Michelle Berriedale-Johnson. Berkeley: University of California Press, 1984.

Dumas on Food: Recipes and Anecdotes from the Classic Grand Dictionnaire de Cuisine, translated by Alan and Jane Davidson. New York: Oxford University Press, 1987.

Alexandre Dumas's Adventures in Czarist Russia, by Alexandre Dumas. Westport: Greenwood Press, 1975. First published by Chilton in 1961.

The Count of Monte Cristo, by Alexandre Dumas. Boston: Little, Brown, 1899. First published in 1844–1845.

Grand Dictionnaire de Cuisine, by Alexandre Dumas. Paris: Alphonse Lemerre, 1873.

Impressions of Travel in Egypt and Arabia Petraea, by Alexandre Dumas. New York: John S. Taylor, 1839.

Propos d'Art et de Cuisine, by Alexandre Dumas. Paris: Calman-Levy, 1877.

Notes Towards the Definition of Culture, by Thomas Stern Eliot. New York: Harcourt Brace Jovanovich, 1949.

The Penny Universities, by Aytoun Ellis. London: Secker & Warburg, 1956.

The Epicure, v. 34, no. 1. Boston, April 1920.

The Escoffier Cookbook: A Guide to the Fine Art of French Cuisine, by Auguste Escoffier. The American edition of *Guide Culinaire,* 1903. New York: Crown, 1969.

Le Guide Culinaire, by Auguste Escoffier. Paris: Flammarion, 1921, 1948.

Le Livre des menus, by Auguste Escoffier. Paris: Ernest Flammarion, 1927.

Acetaria: A Discourse of Sallets, by John Evelyn. New York: Women's Auxiliary Brooklyn Botanical Gardens, 1937. Reprint of the first edition of 1699.

Gastronomical and Culinary Literature, by Barbara L. Feret. London: The Scarecrow Press, 1979.

The History of Tom Jones, a Foundling, by Henry Fielding. London: George Bell & Co., 1907. First published in 1749.

The Journals of Celia Fiennes, edited and with an introduction by Christopher Morris. London: The Cresset Press, 1949, rev. ed., 1947.

How to Cook a Wolf, by M. F. K. Fisher. New York: Duell, Sloan and Pearce, 1942.

Literary Cafés of Paris, by Noël Riley Fitch. Washington and Philadelphia: Starrhill Press, 1989.

A Taste of Scotland, by Theodora FitzGibbon. New York: Avenel Books (division of Crown), 1970.

A Taste of the West Country in Food and in Pictures, by Theodora FitzGibbon. London and Sydney: Pan Books, 1975. First published in 1972 by J. M. Dent & Sons.

Madame Bovary, by Gustave Flaubert, translated by Mildred Marmur. New York: New American Library, 1964. First published in 1857.

New York Is Not America: Being a Mirror to the States, by Ford Madox Ford. New York: Albert & Charles Boni, 1927.

Portraits from Life, by Ford Madox Ford. Chicago: Henry Regnery Company. First published in 1936.

Provence: From Minstrels to the Machine, by Ford Madox Ford. London: J. B. Lippincott Co., 1933.

"Porridge or Prunes, Sir?" by E. M. Forster. *Wine and Food,* v. 21–24, 1939.

Love Letters, edited by John Fostini. New York: Robert Speller & Sons, 1958.

Parnassus Near Piccadilly: An Anthology, edited by Leslie Frewin. London: Leslie Frewin, 1965.

Great Friends, by David Garnett. New York: Atheneum, 1980.

The Haschish Club, by Théophile Gautier. See *Poem of Hashish,* by Charles Baudelaire.

Dorothy Wordsworth, by Robert Gittings and Jo Manton. Oxford: Clarendon Press, 1985.

The Art of Cookery Made Plain and Easy, by Hannah Glasse. London: W. Strahan et al., 1767.

Campaign in France, 1792, by Johann Wolfgang von Goethe. New York: Suhrkamp Publishers, 1987.

The Goncourt Journals, 1851–1870, by Edmond and Jules de Goncourt, edited and translated by Lewis Galantlère. New York: Doubleday, Doran & Co., 1937.

Pages from the Goncourt Journal, by Edmond and Jules de Goncourt, edited and translated by Robert Baldick. London: The Folio Society, 1980. Also London: Oxford University Press, 1962.

Coffee Recipes: Customs, Facts and Fancies, by Jean Gordon. Woodstock: Red Rose Publications, 1963.

Close to Colette: An Intimate Portrait of a Woman of Genius, by Maurice Goudeket. New York: Farrar, Straus & Giroux, 1957.

Balzac in Slippers, by Léon Gozlan. New York: Robert McBridge & Co, 1929. First published in French as *Balzac en pantouffles* in 1862.

A Commonplace Book of Cookery, compiled by Robert Grabhorn. San Francisco: North Point Press, 1985.

Wind in the Willows, by Kenneth Grahame. New York: Viking Press, 1983. First published in 1908.

Émile Zola, by Elliott M. Grant. Boston: Twayne Publishers, 1966.

The Spice of Life, by Sheldon Greenberg and Elisabeth Lambert Ortiz. New York: Amaryllis Press, 1983.

A Sort of Life, by Graham Greene. New York: Simon & Schuster, 1971.

Ways of Escape, by Graham Greene. New York: Simon & Schuster, 1980.

English Food, an anthology chosen by Jane Grigson. London: Macmillan, 1974.

Good Things, by Jane Grigson. New York: Alfred A. Knopf, 1971.

Jane Grigson's Vegetable Book, by Jane Grigson. New York: Atheneum, 1979.

The Observer Guide to British Cookery, by Jane Grigson. London: Michael Joseph, 1984.

Manuel des amphityrons, by Grimod de la Reynière, Alexandre Balthazar Laurent. Paris: Capelle et Renand, 1808.

Coffee Taverns, Cocoa Houses, and Coffee Palaces, by E. Hepple Hall. London: Partridge & Co., 1878.

Lettres au petit corsaire, by Renée Hamon. Paris: Flammarion, 1963.

The Lover's Quotation Book: A Literary Companion, edited by Helen Handley. Wainscott, NY: Pushcart Press, 1986.

The Mayor of Casterbridge, by Thomas Hardy. London: Collins, 1980. First published 1886.

Harper's Magazine, v.144, May 1922, 1867.

The Concise Oxford Companion to American Literature, by James D. Hart. New York: Oxford University Press, 1986.

The Oxford Companion to French Literature, compiled and edited by Sir Paul Harvey and J. E. Heseltine. Oxford: Clarendon Press, 1987.

Passages from the English Notebooks, by Nathaniel Hawthorne. Boston: James R. Osgood & Co., 1871.

Notes in England and Italy, by Mrs. Sofia Hawthorne. New York: G. P. Putnam & Son, 1869.

Eating Together: Recollections and Recipes, by Lillian Hellman and Peter Feibleman. Boston: Little, Brown, 1984.

A Moveable Feast, by Ernest Hemingway. London: Cape, 1964.

Baudelaire the Damned, by F. W. J. Hemmings. New York: Scribner's, 1982.

Convivial Dickens: The Drinks of Dickens and His Times, by Edward Hewett and W. F. Acton. Athens, Ohio: Ohio University Press, 1983.

A Jane Austen Household Book with Martha Lloyd's Recipes, by Peggy Hickman. Newton Abbot: Readers Union Group of Book Clubs, 1978.

"Emily Dickinson's Letters," by Thomas Wentworth Higginson. *The Atlantic Monthly,* October 1891.

The Greedy Book: A Feast for the Eyes, compiled by Brian Hill. London: Rupert Hart Davis, 1966.

The Carlyles at Home, by Thea Holme. London: Oxford University Press, 1965.

A Cup of Tea: An Afternoon Anthology of Fine China and Tea Traditions, edited by Geraldine Holt. New York: Simon & Schuster, 1991.

Food and Drink in America, by Richard Hooker. New York: Bobbs-Merrill, 1981.

The Big Sea: An Autobiography, by Langston Hughes. New York: Alfred A. Knopf, 1945.

Table Talk, by Leigh Hunt. London: Smith Elder & Co., 1851.

Eating and Drinking: An Anthology for Epicures, compiled by Peter Hunt. London: Ebury Press, 1961.

Mules and Men, by Zora Neale Hurston. Bloomington: Indiana University Press, 1935, 1963, 1978.

Their Eyes Were Watching God, by Zora Neale Hurston. Urbana: University of Illinois Press, 1937, 1978.

Literary Landmarks of London, by Laurence Hutton. Boston: James R. Osgood & Co., 1885.

The Savoy: The Romance of a Great Hotel, by Stanley Jackson. London: Frederick Muller, 1964, 1979.

A Little Tour in France, by Henry James. New York: AMS Press, 1975. First published as *En Provence* in *Atlantic Monthly* in 1883–1884.

Emily Dickinson: Friend and Neighbor, by MacGregor Jenkins, Boston: Little, Brown, 1930.

Colette, by Nicole Ward Jouve. Indianapolis: Indiana University Press, 1987.

The Coffee Cookbook, by William I. Kaufman. New York: Doubleday, 1964.

Garden of Zola: Émile Zola and His Novels for English Readers, by Graham King. New York: Schocken, 1983.

The Chocolate Lover's Companion, by Norman Kolpas. New York: Quick Fox, 1977.

Purely for Pleasure, by Margaret Lane. London: Hamish Hamilton, 1966.

Larousse Gastronomique, edited by Jenifer Harvey Lang. New York: Crown, 1984.

The Illustrated Pepys: From the Diary, selected and edited by Robert Latham. Berkley: University of California Press, 1983.

The Pleasure of Your Company: A History of Manners and Meals, by Jean Latham. London: Adams & Charles Black, 1972.

Flowers in the Blood: The Story of Opium, by Dean Latimer and Jeff Goldberg. New York: Franklin Watts, 1981.

"The Decay of the Cook," by Jacques Le Clerq. *American Mercury,* v. 6, October 1925.

Cider with Rosie, by Laurie Lee. London: Penguin, 1990. First published in 1959.

Colette: A Biographical Study, by Maria Le Hardouin, translated by Erik De Mauny. London: Staples Press Ltd., 1958.

Literary Neighborhoods of New York, by Marcia Leisner. Washington and Philadelphia: Starrhill Press, 1989.

"The Culinary Triangle," by Claude Lévi-Strauss. *Partisan Review,* v. 33, 1966.

The Chronicles of Narnia, by C.S. Lewis. New York: Macmillan, 1951–1956.

With Love from Gracie, by Grace Hegger Lewis. New York: Harcourt, Brace & Co., 1951, 1955.

The Best of A. J. Liebling, selected by William Cole. London: Methuen, 1965.

London Coffee Houses, by Bryant Lillywhite. London: George Allen & Unwin Ltd., 1963.

Paris: A Literary Companion, by Ian Littlewood. New York: Harper & Row, 1988.

How Green Was My Valley, by Richard Llewellyn. New York: Macmillan, 1940.

The Left Bank: Writers, Artists, and Politics from the Popular Front to the Cold War, by Herbert Lottman. Boston: Houghton Mifflin, 1982.

John Dos Passos: A Twentieth Century Odyssey, by Townsend Luddington. New York: E. P. Dutton, 1980.

The Herb Book, by John Lust. New York: Bantam Books, 1987.

The Ballad of the Sad Café, by Carson McCullers. Boston: Houghton Mifflin, 1987. First published in 1951.

On Food and Cooking: The Science and Law of the Kitchen, by Harold McGee. New York: Scribner's, 1984.

Macauley's History of England, by Thomas Babington Macauley. New York: E. P. Dutton, 1972. First published in 1849.

The Savoy of London, by Compton Mackenzie. London: George G. Harrap & Co., 1953.

Journal of Katherine Mansfield, edited by J. Middleton Murry. New York: Alfred A. Knopf, 1946.

Byron: A Portrait, by Leslie Marchand. New York: Alfred A. Knopf, 1970.

Lord Byron: Selected Letters and Journals, edited by Leslie Marchand. Cambridge: Belknap Press of Harvard University Press, 1982.

Melmoth the Wanderer, by Charles Robert Maturin. Lincoln: University of Nebraska Press, 1961. First published in 1820.

A Writer's Notebook, by William Somerset Maugham. New York: Doubleday, 1949.

The Titans: A Three Generation Biography of the Dumas, by André Maurois. New York: Harper & Brothers, 1957.

The World of Marcel Proust, by André Maurois, translated by Moura Budberg. New York: Harper & Row, 1974.

Literary Villages of London, by Luree Miller. Washington and Philadelphia: Starrhill Press, 1989.

Remember to Remember, by Henry Miller. New York: New Directions, 1947.

The House at Pooh Corner, by A. A. Milne. London: Methuen, 1928.

Sweetness and Power: The Place of Sugar in Modern History, by Sidney W. Mintz. New York: Viking/Elisabeth Sifton Books, 1985.

Byron's Life, Letters, and Journals with Notices of His Life, by Thomas Moore. London: John Murray, 1839.

Chocolate: An Illustrated History, by Marcia and Frederic Morton. New York: Crown, 1986.

The Spice of Love: Wisdom and Wit About Love Through the Ages, selected by Robert Myers. Kansas City: Hallmark Cards, Inc., 1968.

Dining with Proust, by Jean-Bernard Naudin, Anne Borrel, and Alain Senderens. New York: Random House, 1992.

Recollections of Virginia Woolf by Her Contemporaries, edited by Joan Russell Noble. London: Penguin, 1975.

The Art and Magic of Cooking, by Raymond Oliver, translated by Ambrose Heath. London: Frederick Muller, 1959.

Coming Up for Air, by George Orwell. London: Secker & Warburg, 1986. First published in 1939.

Down and Out in Paris and London, by George Orwell. London: Secker & Warburg, 1986. First published in 1933.

Road to Wigan Pier, by George Orwell. New York: Harcourt Brace & World, 1958.

Table Talk on Books, Men, and Manners, by Robert Conger Pell. New York: Putnam & Co., 1853.

The Illustrated Pepys, Extracts from the Diary, selected and edited by Robert Latham. Los Angeles: University of California Press, 1983.

Crazy Like a Fox, by S. J. Perelman. New York: Random House, 1944 (fourth printing).

La Cuisine Provençale, by Henri Philippon. Paris: Robert Laffont, 1966.

Baudelaire, by Claude Pichois, translated by Graham Robb. London: Hamish Hamilton, 1989.

Cafe Royal Days, by Captain Nichols Pigache. London: Hutchinson, 1934.

Eat the Grapes Downward: An Uninhibited Romp through the Surprising World of Food, by Vernon Pizer. New York: Dodd, Mead & Co., 1983.

Selected Tales, by Edgar Allan Poe. London: Oxford University Press, 1991. "The Cask of Amontillado," first published in 1846.

Samuel Pepys, by Arthur Ponsonby. New York: Book League of America, 1929.

"Bon Mots" for Menus, by E. Cox Price. London: Practical Press, 1936.

Swann's Way, by Marcel Proust. New York: Holt & Co., 1925.

Consuming Passions: Being an Historic Inquiry into Certain English Appetites, by Philippa Pullar. Boston: Little, Brown, 1970.

Paris Was Our Mistress: Memoirs of a Lost and Found Generation, by Samuel Putnam. New York: Viking, 1947.

Casanova in London, by Peter Quennell. New York: Stein & Day, 1971.

The Life of Langston Hughes, v. 1: 1902–1941: *I, Too, Sing America,* by Arnold Rampersand. New York: Oxford University Press, 1986.

The Gourmet's Companion, edited by Cyril Ray. London: Eyre & Spottiswoode, 1963.

The London Ritz Book of Christmas, by Jennie Reekie. London: Ebury Press, 1989.

La République des lettres, April 13, 1877.

Colette, by Joanna Richardson. New York: Franklin Watts, 1984.

Letters to a Young Poet, by Rainer Maria Rilke, translated by M. D. Herter Norton. New York: Norton, 1934, 1962.

Samuel Rogers and His Circle, by R. Elis Roberts. London: Methuen & Co., 1910.

Wilkie Collins, by Kenneth Robinson. London: David-Poynter, 1974. First published in 1951.

Recollections of the Table-Talk of Samuel Rogers. London: Edward Moxon, 1856.

The Food of France, by Waverly Root. New York: Alfred A. Knopf, 1970.

The Food of Italy, by Waverly Root. New York: Atheneum, 1971.

Cyrano de Bergerac, by Edmond Rostand, translated into English verse by Brian Hooker. New York: Bantam Books, 1988. First published 1898.

"Colette and Wine," by Alice Wooledge Salman. *Journal of Gastronomy,* v. 1, no. 3, 1985.

Honoré de Balzac: His Life and Writings, by Mary F. Sandars. London: Stanley Paul & Co., 1904, 1914.

Dinner with Tom Jones: Eighteenth-century Cookery Adapted for the Modern Kitchen, by Lorna J. Sass. New York: Metropolitan Museum of Art, 1977.

Le Répertoire de La Cuisine, by Louis Saulnier. New York: Barron's, 1976.

Will You Marry Me? Proposal Letters of Seven Centuries, edited by Helene Scheu-Riesz. New York: Island Working Press, 1940.

The Greedy Book, by Frank Schloesser. London: Gay and Bird, 1906.

Never Satisfied: A Cultural History of Diets, Fantasies, and Fat, by Hillel Schwartz. New York: Doubleday, 1986.

The Epicure's Companion, edited by Ann Serrane and John Tebbel. New York: David McKay Co., 1962.

Letters from Madame la Marquise de Sévigné, selected, translated, and introduced by Violet Hamersly. London: Secker & Warburg, 1955.

Romantic Rebel: The Life and Times of George Sand, by Felicia Seyd. New York: Viking, 1940.

The Gastronomic Regenerator, by Monsieur A. Soyer. London: John Ollivier, 1849.

The Spectator. #403, June 12, 1712. Complete in two volumes. Philadelphia: J. J. Woodward. 1832.

Baudelaire, by Enid Starkie. New York: New Directions, 1958.

Flaubert in Egypt, translated and edited by Frances Steegmuller. London: The Bodley Head, 1972.

The Pooh Cookbook: Inspired by Winnie-the-Pooh and The House at Pooh Corner by A.A. Milne, recipes by Katie Stewart. London: Methuen Children's Books, 1971.

And So To Dine: A Brief Account of the Food and Drink of Mr. Pepys Based on His Diary, by S. A. E. Ström. London: Frederick Books, 1955.

Directions to Servants and Other Pieces in Prose and Verse, by Jonathan Swift. Dublin: George Faulkner, 1752, v. 8.

Journal to Stella, (1710–1713) by Jonathan Swift. London: G. Bell & Sons, 1924.

The Prose Works of Jonathan Swift, v. iv, *A Proposal for Correcting the English Tongue, Polite Conversation, etc.* "Hints Towards an Essay on Conversation." Oxford: Basil Blackwell, 1957.

Food in History, by Reay Tannahill, revised and updated edition. New York: Crown, 1988.

Recollections of Guy de Maupassant, by François Tassart, translated by Mina Round. London: The Bodley Head, 1912.

Tatler, Volume the First, London, 1804.

William Makepeace Thackeray: Contributions to the Morning Chronicle, edited by Gordon N. Ray. London and Urbana: University of Illinois Press, 1966.

Is Sex Necessary?, by James Thurber and E. B. White. New York and London: Harper & Brothers, 1929.

Clubs and Club Life in London, by John Timbs. London: John Camden Hotten, 1872.

The Alice B. Toklas Cook Book, by Alice B. Toklas. London: Penguin, 1961. First published by Michael Joseph in 1954.

The Food Book, by James Trager. New York: Grossmans Publishers, 1970.

Miss Mackenzie, by Anthony Trollope. New York: Arno Press, 1981. First published in 1865.

North America, by Anthony Trollope. New York: Harper & Brothers, 1862.

Paris and the Parisians, by Frances Trollope. London: Richard Bentley, 1836.

Domestic Manners of the Americans, by Frances Trollope. London: Whittaker Treacher & Co., 1832.

The Household Cookery Book, by Félix Urbain-Dubois. London: Longman, Green & Co., 1871.

La Cuisine de Tous les Pays, by Félix Urbain-Dubois. Paris: E. Flammarion, 12th edition, 1926.

Nouvelle Cuisine Bourgeoise: Pour La Ville et pour La Campagne, by Félix Urbain-Dubois. 3rd edition, 1882.

An Englishman in Paris, by Albert D. Vandam. New York: D. Appleton & Co., 1892.

Much Depends on Dinner, by Margaret Visser. Penguin, 1989.

The Secret History of the Calves-Head Club, by Edward Ward. London: B. Bragge, 1706.

When the Going Was Good, by Evelyn Waugh. London: Penguin, 1946. First published in 1929.

Cather's Kitchens: Foodways in Literature and Life, by Roger L. and Linda K. Welsch. Lincoln: University of Nebraska Press, 1987.

A Backward Glance, by Edith Wharton. New York: D. Appleton & Company, 1934.

French Ways and Their Meaning, by Edith Wharton. New York: D. Appleton & Company, 1919.

Plays, by Oscar Wilde. New York: Norton, 1983.

Great Cooks and Their Recipes, by Anne Willan. Boston: Little, Brown, 1992.

Food and Drink in Britain, by C. Anne Wilson. London: Constable, 1973.

A Room of One's Own, by Virginia Woolf. New York: Harcourt Brace Jovanovitch, 1929, 1957.

A Writer's Diary: Being Extracts from the Diary of Virginia Woolf, edited by Leonard Woolf. London: Hogarth Press, 1953.

To the Lighthouse, by Virginia Woolf. New York: Harcourt Brace Jovanovich, 1927.

The Grasmere Journals, by Dorothy Wordsworth, edited by Pamela Woolf. Oxford: Clarendon Press, 1991.

A Memoir of Honoré de Balzac, compiled and written by Katharine Prescott Wormeley. Boston: Roberts Brothers, 1892.

"Emily Dickinson as Cook and Poetess," by Helen Wyman. *Better Food,* June 1906.

La Belle Lisa or The Paris Market Girls (Le Ventre de Paris), by Émile Zola. Philadelphia: T. B. Peterson & Bros., 1882.

Nana, by Émile Zola. New York: Three Sirens Press, 1933.

Balzac, by Stefan Zweig, translated by William and Dorothy Rose. New York: Viking, 1946.

V

Vanilla Cream, 136
Victoria Sandwiches, 101–102

Y

Yorkshire Pudding, 100